The Shadow's Fall

Siara Brandt

For B.

Prologue

It was the dead of winter, the final breath of a dying day. Dusk came early under a brooding sky while the earth grew hushed and heavy with its secrets.

Snow fell. A profoundly silent thing, it transformed the woods surrounding the old farmhouse. Silent also, starkly-defined trees reached bare arms to a gray, forbidding sky.

The slow drift of snowflakes was already clinging to skeletal branches that were reflected in the glass of empty windows. Through dust-veiled, distorted panes the last of daylight filtered, though faintly, to become the ghost that lingered in a man's eyes.

He stood motionless now that it was done. Still rigid with the rage that had consumed him, every muscle of his body was tensed. Every nerve was strained. His eyes had a vacant look to them as he drew himself inward, for a brief space of time, to a place only he ever went.

His mouth, almost always taut with bitterness, was drawn even further back against his teeth, until it seemed that his face was frozen in some hideous death grin. There was no smile, in him, however. Nor was there regret. Regret, if it came at all, would come later. For now, his thoughts were for himself. Survival loomed uppermost in those thoughts.

He mentally shook himself and refocused. His gaze swept the room for signs of his presence. He saw none. He turned his head slowly, eyes narrowing as he listened, but he was aware only of the heavy silence that had descended upon the empty rooms of the farmhouse.

1

The silence had suddenly grown oppressive. It seemed to surround him with a presence all its own. In spite of himself, he sent a quick, searching glance down the darkening hallway behind him. He saw nothing, save, for a moment, a familiar picture that held his gaze.

Dark, intricately-carved wood, chipped and scratched with age, framed a violent hunting scene. The blood and the terror of the kill were vividly portrayed in deep and somber hues. Old hues cracked and yellowed by time. It was a picture that had always fascinated him.

A sudden gust of wind rattled the windows. The unexpected sound made him start, caused the involuntary scraping of one boot heel against the worn floorboards. Both sounds were harsh intrusions that jarred his already tightly-strung nerves.

It would be nightfall soon. A deeper coldness would come creeping in with the darkness. Already the rising wind invaded every crack and crevice in the old house. It made its way, unseen, past every doorway and down each hall. It caused a sudden chill to seep down to the marrow of his bones as well. He released his breath in a hushed and vile oath, his eyes still searching. It was as if something already haunted the place.

Belief in ghosts and hauntings had been part of his heritage. It was something too deeply ingrained to be ignored or dismissed. He cursed again, more profanely this time, and looked back at the dim interior of the closet.

There was a steady drip of blood from the calloused fingers of the outstretched hand. A dark pool of it had already seeped out from under the stitched edge of the wool blanket. It crept along the floorboards and saturated the old, rose-patterned carpet in an ever-widening stain.

No sense to try and conceal anything now. The blood would show even with the closet door closed. There would be a lot of blood, he knew, before there was no more left to drain from the body.

His thoughts shifted suddenly, as they were wont to do. He had never had much control over them. He had a sudden, vivid recollection of each shot. There had been five of them. He recalled the expression of shock that he had seen in the eyes that were now staring sightlessly up into the deeply-shadowed, upper reaches of the closet. Pale eyes. Pale as ice on a pond in winter. Nearly a reflection of his own.

He had felt rage at the accusation in those eyes. Rage and more that he hadn't let himself identify. He had not thought the thing through.

He had merely reacted. And that reaction had been like a wildfire that had leapt beyond his ability to control it. It had been consuming. Devastating. Deadly. Such was the power of rage. He knew this from the past. Rage was a destroying emotion.

He remembered every detail with a strange clarity. He remembered waiting for death to come. He had even grown impatient waiting. But death had come at last. There could be no other outcome. And yet it seemed that those eyes accused him still.

He had a sudden impulse to kick the blanket over the damning accusation still staring out from those unblinking eyes. But for some reason, he could not make himself cross the room. Daylight still filtered in through the tall windows, though weakly. It was enough illumination, however, to see that the familiar face had a pallor that was already becoming ghastly.

His own face took on an ashen hue, for, as he stood there with the darkness deepening around him, he was suddenly aware of the smell of blood. It was not an unfamiliar smell. Hunting was a passion with him. It always had been. He had killed and butchered countless animals over the years. He had been trained to it from early childhood. But this odor seemed different somehow. It was pervasive, a thing that unaccountably sickened him. It seemed that as he breathed it into his body, it became a part of him.

It caused him to draw faintly back against the door jamb with the gun still gripped tightly in his hand. It was true that he had killed before. But it had never been like this.

Something biblical, though fleeting, tried to take root in his mind, threatened to grow to uncontrollable proportions. He forced it back down. Such thoughts were imperfect concepts in any case, to be used most often to control or to justify, though he, himself, did not understand the danger of such distortions. He would work through those things later, in his own way.

He was amazed to find that he was trembling. He frowned, a fierce intensity etching his features now. He was also aware, deep inside him, of another tiny, but stubborn flame that was in danger of being fanned into something much bigger. It was a thing to be fought as well. He succeeded in smothering the flame and was able, by degrees, to replace it with a greater portion of the shadow that had long ago begun to darken his heart. Still, for a helpless space of time, he remained rooted there, poised on the knife edge of something that threatened to drag him downward into the depths of some dark, oppressive whirlpool.

He fought it. He refused to let the past beckon. He was not willing to allow the weakness. Anger kept him focused. Anger was a familiar emotion, one that could be more easily directed outward.

Bitterness curled his lips. Life was not fair. Life was hard. Granite-hard and, more often than not, unchangeable. He knew this. He accepted it. And more important than that, he was smart enough to expect it. He had lived with misery and cruelty all his life. From the very beginning, brutality had been etched into his existence. It was what he knew. He had learned to fight back with the thing that had been carved most deeply into him. His own brand of brutality. Carefully nurtured over the years, it became a survival of sorts. It became a way to work through some of the things that had surrounded him every day of his life since birth.

To exist in the shadow of such untruths, he needed lies. The same lies embraced by untold generations before him. The same ones so unconditionally taught year after hopelessly brutal year.

Those lies had already sunk greedy claws deeply into his soul, tearing at his moral fiber one bloody shred at a time. And yet he clung to those lies like a desperate man clings to a sinking life raft, one who is too afraid to let go and lean on something more substantial.

"You should have let it the hell alone," he muttered, justifying. "You would have had it spread all over the damned place. And then where would we have been?"

He shook his head slightly in the direction of the darkness now wreathing the unmoving form beneath the blanket. Hadn't he understood the consequences? Hadn't he realized what revelation meant? For all of them?

"Fool," he whispered passionately as he shook his head, immediately feeling foolish himself for speaking out loud to a dead man.

He was able to console himself with the knowledge that he had silenced the damning words forever. He understood secrets. Just as he understood threats. He had lived in the shadow of both all his life. Because to know was to question and to question was to disobey. He had been taught to obey. Unconditionally. Unthinkingly.

His jaw went outward in a vicious thrust. The thing had been done. There was no sense going over it. There was no time for regrets. Nor weakness. He even began to convince himself that he possessed a superior strength because, as had seemed to be the case for as long as he could remember, he had to be the one to take care of the unpleasant tasks that no one else had a stomach for. He even prided himself that cunning and ability to act in difficult situations were among his strengths. His virtues.

His mouth curled bitterly. Had there ever been anyone, ever, who had looked out for him? The answer was a dull, hard-as-nails truth. No. He had only had himself. And so, accustomed to thinking of himself first, he considered his own survival.

He crossed the bedroom, making sure to avoid the blood, careful not to leave footprints. His boot steps were muted on the worn carpet as he went around to the opposite side of the iron bedstead. His eyes narrowed as he surveyed the furniture in the room.

Every piece of furniture, here and throughout the entire house, upstairs and down, was an old hand-me-down. Everything he had ever grown up around was a reminder of poverty. They had all become so accustomed to it that they never even noticed it all around them. There was, however, one thing of value here.

He pulled the drawer of the small bedside table open and found what he was looking for. Opening the worn-thin, gray cloth sack, he closed his fist around the coins and put them in his pocket. He reached into the sack again, fished out the last coins and pocketed them as well, then tossed the empty sack onto the bed.

He pushed the drawer shut. He had to shove it hard to get it past the point where it stuck. That was the way it was with all junk furniture, he thought fiercely as the drawer slammed shut.

Without another backward glance, he left the room and moved down the dark hallway, ignoring the distorted image of himself in the old oval mirror that was hanging at the end of the stairwell.

Downstairs, he opened the kitchen door and stood looking out into the cold February night. He shivered as the wind bit through his unbuttoned coat. The snow was coming thicker and faster now. The wind was rising. It was beginning to drive the snow across the bare field behind the house. It was the kind of night most people would stay at home and keep indoors, he thought. Luck seemed to be on his side.

His gaze shifted and fixed on the highway. He stepped back suddenly so that he would not be silhouetted in the doorway and stared intently as two headlights probed the darkness. He remained frozen there as the twin beacons touched field and forest with strangely-shifting, elongated shapes in a surreal landscape of falling snow.

He turned his face to the window across the kitchen behind him and continued to watch the progress of the car on the highway. But the car passed by and no further movement, no sounds or signs of life, came from any direction.

He stepped outside and pulled the door closed behind him, giving it a final jerk when it stuck. With the wariness of a prisoner in flight, he started across the snow-swept field. Worried that another car might come along the highway, he hurried towards the line of fence posts that jutted darkly out of the ground. Like a row of headstones, they showed starkly against the pale gleam of snow.

Flight consumed him now. Fear-driven, he quickened his pace towards the dark, solid mass of forest at the far end of the field until he was almost running. Everything remained silent save for the faint, whispered moan of the wind in the trees and the snow crunching softly underfoot.

The cold wind stung his face and snow hissed in the darkness all around him. But the snow would, he calculated, begin to blot out his footprints even before he reached the concealing darkness of the woods beyond the boundary of fence. He almost smiled at his luck. There would be no trace of his presence left behind.

Chapter 1

13 years later

"We may be dealing with a serial killer here."

Silence followed the soberly-spoken words. All eyes remained fixed on the dark-haired man sitting at the long wooden table that dominated the room.

The big man standing at the center of the wall of tall, arched windows slowly turned. With tawny eyebrows raised, he stared intently at the speaker as if he was expecting, perhaps, the punchline to some preposterous joke.

"A serial killer?" he echoed, his brows now drawing together in a frown. "By God," he breathed in disbelief. "You're serious."

Deputy Baran Prichard gave a faint, scoffing snort before he stepped away from the windows and walked around the table to pour himself another cup of coffee. He slowly stirred sugar into his cup and said, "You may be used to the kinds of things where you come from. But this is Alder Grove, not Chicago."

A slightly sarcastic smile curled one corner of the deputy's mouth as he lifted his cup to his mouth. He didn't bother to hide the smile before he took a careful sip of the steaming coffee, still watching the other man over the styrofoam rim.

The deputy lowered his cup, grimacing as he swallowed, and spoke again. "Two murders more than a year apart seems like the work of a serial killer to you? We have no evidence, absolutely nothing, that tells us that these murders are connected."

"Actually, we do."

Jenna Maurin, who was also seated at the table, had been watching the deputy and now she looked at Jesse Logan. The late morning sunlight falling through the tall windows gleamed on hair black as a raven's wing. Hair worn too long for Alder Grove standards. There was a slight frown on Jesse's face as he reached for the folder that lay on the table before him.

"The initial examination of the body indicated that the victim's wrists had been bound," Jesse said as he opened the folder. "The bruising and the lacerations also indicate that he same type of rope was used and that this victim was suspended in the same manner before death as Calia Devoss was a year ago."

The deputy was far from being convinced. Deputy Baran Prichard, known as Bear by those who knew him, was a tall man, standing over six feet tall. Broad-shouldered and well-muscled in spite of a slightly rounded idle bulging beneath his tan uniform shirt, he was a well-known presence representing law and order in the town. He had lived in Alder Grove his entire life and knew practically everyone in the farming community. He even farmed part time himself.

Right now the deputy was an imposing shadow that blocked out a good portion of the sunlight falling through the window behind him. "Come on," he said. "This is Alder Grove, for God sakes. The only crime we have had in the past three months is Cletus Doyle's dogs running loose and a snake down in Ivadell Bishop's cistern."

Jesse gave a patient nod of agreement, ignoring the deputy's frown. "That's true," Jesse went on. "But the examination also revealed extensive cuts and lacerations on the bottoms of the victim's feet. Her shoes were on, however. Calia Devoss was found with the same kinds of marks. Both of her shoes were also on."

The deputy was still skeptical. His face showed it as he crossed his arms over his broad chest. With a glance towards the open door and the hallway beyond it to make sure that they were not overheard, he said in a lowered voice. "I thought that unofficially we had decided that Ferd Devoss had killed his wife because she was going to leave him. Any anyway," he continued to argue. "The two women were killed in different ways."

"That's also true," Jesse said. "Calia Devoss was shot while this latest victim was stabbed. But it isn't uncommon for serial killers to use different methods. He may be fine tuning his method.

8

"Both women also had similar bruising on their throats," Jesse went on. "And with evidence of petechial hemorrhaging in the eyes, I am pretty certain that when we get the final autopsy report on this victim, we will find that she was strangled before she was killed. Not enough to cause death, but enough possibly to cause unconsciousness. Which is another thing the victims have in common.

"In any case, there are enough similarities here," He made a slight gesture with his hand to indicate the papers before him. "To make us seriously consider the possibility that this is the work of the same person."

Jesse settled back in his chair and Jenna saw that he was serious. Very serious. And aside from Bear Prichard, he was being taken seriously by the other three people in the room, two more deputies and a dispatcher who had come in that morning after hearing about the murder.

It had been an early morning for all of them after receiving word that a woman's body had been found in the woods in a shallow grave just east of the old Presbyterian Church cemetery. Jesse had been called to the scene sometime before daylight. He had gotten back to the station about an hour ago.

Jesse Logan, unlike Bear Prichard, had moved to Alder Grove only a little over a year ago. He had come from Chicago where he had worked as a detective for the Chicago Police Department. He had studied criminal psychology and behavior and had some training in forensics which was completely beyond the experience of local law officers. And even though Deputy Prichard would be the last to admit it, there was a grudging respect for Jesse's professional knowledge and experience. Over the past year, everyone in the Alder Grove Police Department had come to respect his opinions because they had always proven to be accurate and reliable. And he seemed very sure of what he was saying right now.

Scowling down at the table before him, Deputy Prichard dragged a hand across the lower half of his face, hesitating a moment before he said, "Yeah, but a *serial killer*?"

Further discussion stopped as the front door to the courthouse opened. Everyone waited as footsteps approached on the checkered marble floor of the main hallway.

Sheriff Lydell Wade entered the room. He removed some papers from a single manila envelope he had been carrying. He tossed both the papers and the envelope onto the center of the table. Without speaking, the sheriff pulled out a chair and took a seat at the table. Still silent, he took off his glasses and polished them slowly before he put them back on. He looked worn out, as if he hadn't slept at all the night before.

"I'm afraid we have a bad situation here. Worse than we thought," he said with a sober look around at each person in the room. "At this point, the victim's ID is official. It was Jana Calder, the daughter of Faye and Bill Calder."

"Hell," Bear Prichard breathed from across the room. He was still standing before the windows, facing the room and shaking his head as if he couldn't believe what he had just heard.

The sheriff sat forward, leaned over the table and cleared his throat. "I have just come from talking to the family. This has hit them hard. As you can imagine." He paused, the lines about his mouth becoming more pronounced. "No," he corrected soberly. "I don't think any of us can imagine what it is like for them."

"I remember coaching Jana in softball years ago," Bear said. "She had to be what? Twenty-three or -four?"

The sheriff compressed his lips for a moment before he quietly replied, "Twenty-two. We won't have all the pathology repots back for a while, but preliminary reports indicate that Jana was tied at the wrists and hung from a tree before she died. The same as Calia Devoss was a year ago. It is looking like we may have a repeat killer on the loose out there."

During the silence that followed his words, the sheriff frowned down at the papers before him. "There were rope fibers along with tree bark embedded in the skin of both women. There would be blood stains on the rope if we had it. But we don't. We also don't have a murder weapon. Which would be a gun in the Devoss case and a knife in this latest killing. And so far no clues that could lead us to a suspect or a motive."

The sheriff paused and released a deep sigh before he went on. "Cyril Clayton had been out coon hunting when he discovered the body. Or rather when his dog discovered the body. He has no alibi for the time the killing probably took place. Technically, Cyril was trespassing and hunting on private property where he shouldn't have been, but I think everyone in this room will agree that while Blue is something of an oddball, he's no killer."

No one commented except for Bear who gave a low grunt of agreement.

10

"Both women were partially clothed," the sheriff continued. "Calia Devoss had been shot- " He paused, picking up the top sheet of paper and reading through the report before him. "Six times. Four of which could have caused immediate or eventual death. Jana Calder had been stabbed. Cause of death is not yet officially known but we don't need a report to tell us that her death probably resulted from multiple stab wounds. Though it's true that we don't have the autopsy report yet to tell us exactly how she died or how many stab wounds there were, there were more wounds than were necessary to cause death. A clear case of overkill." He looked up. "Isn't that what it's called, Jes?"

"Yes," Jesse replied. "These were definitely premeditated killings committed by what is called an organized killer. Someone who carefully plans everything out ahead of time. Someone who puts a lot of thought into it. An organized killer often commits the actual murder in one place and then moves the body to another location. He then removes everything from the scene to make sure no evidence is left behind."

Jesse frowned thoughtfully as he continued. "You could call these cold-blooded killings, but there was a lot of hate and rage behind them."

The sheriff got up to pour himself a cup of coffee. He slid back down into his seat and listened carefully as Jesse went on.

"Because he tied and suspended his victims from trees – they were clearly alive at that point – my guess is that he wanted them to feel helpless. Their shoes were removed, along with part of their clothing which would have made them feel even more helpless and vulnerable. Our perpetrator has a need to feel control. And power. Lots of it. About par for the course for these kinds of crimes."

Sheriff Wade nodded slowly, his eyes narrowing in recollection. "I remember thinking that it was odd how Calia Devoss had the bottoms of her feet all tore to hell even though she had her shoes on."

"Most likely their shoes were removed sometime before they died," Jesse said. "And replaced again after they were killed. It's hard to tell exactly why, but it would make them more vulnerable, maybe make it harder for them to escape because it would slow them down. Calia Devoss had done some running in bare feet over rough ground to account for her wounds. And I am sure forensics is going to bear this out in this case as well. It's unlikely that both women would have found an opportunity to escape before they were killed. Unless- "

Jesse paused. "The killer let both of them think they were going to get away. Made a cat and mouse game of it. A hunt."

"He hunted them," the sheriff repeated, frowning down at the steaming coffee cup cradled in his hands as he considered the gravity of what they were dealing with. Alder Grove was a rural community. Almost everyone hunted.

Both men glanced up when Bear interjected his own thoughts. "Just what kind of sick bastard hunts and kills women for the fun of it?"

The sheriff looked at Jesse. "I'm wondering that myself. Based on the information we have, can you put together any kind of profile?" he wanted to know.

"There are some basic traits common to most serial killers," Jesse replied as he picked up a pencil and tapped it thoughtfully on the table before him. "As I said before, our perpetrator has a need to be in control of his victims, both physically and mentally. Terror would be one method of attaining a sense of absolute power. He would have issues with feeling out of control himself and this would stem from early childhood. He would almost certainly have been abused himself early in life and as a result he is carrying a great deal of rage from the past when, at some point, he felt powerless and under the control of others. It's safe to assume that he has lived a life of pent-up rage and frustration and that somewhere along the line he has decided that killing is a way to relieve some of his internal tension.

"The circumstances would be different in each case, but when certain conditions are present during early emotional development, some people learn to convert bottled up rage and frustration into sexual tension. It can then become an outlet for displaced hostility and aggression. It's probable that Calia Devoss was sexually assaulted by a stranger before she died, in spite of what her husband told us. It is also likely that this latest victim was assaulted as well. If our killer is using murder as a means of sexual release, it's possible that he has been sexually assaulting women for years. Some repeat killers start as serial rapists, sometimes attacking dozens, even hundreds of victims before they progress to murder. Serial killers are not created overnight.

"But the real high, the real goal here, is power," Jesse went on. "The ultimate power of life over death is what he's after. It may be that some even in the killer's current life has set him off. It may be that he is dealing with something that stirs up the same out-of-control feelings he felt as a child. Most certainly he was exposed to violence early in his life and has adopted it as a way of dealing with his problems. It may have even become part of his survival.

"It's hard to say what has put him over the edge, but he has crossed the point of no return. He can't go backwards, and we have," Jesse continued very soberly. "A very volatile, very dangerous, very driven individual who will kill again if we don't stop him."

"Any way to know how long it may be before he kills again?" the sheriff asked.

"Unfortunately, it's impossible to say at this point, Dell," Jesse answered. "There is what is known as an emotional cooling off period between murders which can span days, months or even years."

It wasn't what the sheriff wanted to hear. He sat silent, staring at his hands which were now laced together on the table before him.

Deputy Prichard, who had also taken a seat at the table, asked, "So what do we do now? Just wait until we have another victim on our hands?"

"No," Jesse replied. "We try and solve this before there are more murders. We start by combing through every piece of evidence available to us. A good place to start is by investigating known sex offenders in the area. And anyone else with a history of violence, particularly against women. We search for any connection between the two victims, then track what they did, who they were with, and find out everything we can, whether it seems relevant or not, in the hours and weeks leading up to their deaths, and see if we can't determine some pattern or basis for selection.

"We also need to study a map. It would be a good idea to check a radius of the surrounding counties to see if there have been other killings that might be related. And any sexual assaults or disappearances that haven't been solved. I suggest we go back at least ten years. Repeat killers often operate for years before anyone realizes what's going on. We have two victims that we know of. The problem is that we don't know when he started killing. There may be more bodies out there that haven't been found.

"The lab results will give us more information. Traces of some sort of gravel-like material were found on this latest victim's body. It appears to be the same substance that was noted in the files on Calia Devoss. It might tell us something about the murder location or where he takes the women before he kills them. And that could be an important step in solving these murders. No one is perfect and serial

13

killers are no exception. Somewhere along the line, he's made a mistake. Or he will make a mistake."

"If this is the work of a serial killer, it could have been done by an outsider," Bear suggested.

"We can't rule out that possibility," Jesse agreed, his gaze following the deputy as he rose and walked to the window.

"I have lived here my whole life," Bear went on as he stared out the window, scanning the town square below. "I can't imagine that someone capable of murder might be walking the streets right now."

He turned back to the room and jammed his hands into his pockets. "Well, what do we do? What are our options if – and I'm not saying I agree with your theories – if there is a serial killer out there? We're responsible for keeping people safe. How do we go about doing that without causing widespread panic? I mean, word of this has probably leaked out already. No doubt this is going to make headlines on the front page of the paper on Tuesday morning."

"It will," Sheriff Wade agreed as he gathered up the papers before him. "I've already talked to Harlan at the paper. I've satisfied him for now with a few details and told him that we are still investigating and looking for the killer. That alone should put people on the alert. At the present time I think that's the best we can do. We don't want the killer to be aware of all the information that we have. H's got us guessing, but let's keep hm guessing, too."

Chapter 2

Jenna looked up at the pavilion that dominated the tree-lined town square. It was a large, ornate structure with tall concrete columns, a tiled roof and elaborate architectural detail. The sidewalks leading up to the pavilion from all sides of the square and the neatly-trimmed grass were dappled with shifting patterns from the heavy canopy of leaves that were moving in the slight breeze. A black wrought iron fence kept the boundaries of the park defined.

There had been a week of mild, spring-like weather. The sun was shining in a clear blue sky. The birds were singing in the huge catalpa trees that shaded the park and the wooden bench where Jenna was finishing her lunch.

There were a few other people taking advantage of the warm weather and having lunch in the park. Several children were playing a boisterous game of tag around some budding lilac bushes. A small black dog was trying to play with them. A young mother with two small children in tow and another woman pushing a baby buggy were shopping at the farmer's market which was dong business along the west side of the square, as it did every Wednesday and Friday.

It was a peaceful scene, a serene reflection of small town life. Everyone going about their business as usual. A quiet park in a quiet town.

Jenna gathered her wrappers and her napkin and stuffed them into the empty paper bag setting on the bench beside her. There were two restaurants in town. Neither of them served fast food and both restaurants were always crowded during the noon rush hour. On days like this when the weather was good, she had gotten into the habit of eating lunch in the park with Jesse, both of them preferring to have lunch here rather than fight the crowds.

The park was right outside the courthouse where they both worked and it made more sense eating together than eating alone. There was an unspoken understanding between them. No dating and no romantic involvement. Jenna had just gotten out of a bad marriage followed by an unpleasant divorce. She had no desire to get tangled up with someone new. And Jesse was still adjusting to major changes in his own life. He had moved to Alder Grove only a year ago, stepping in to raise his sister's two children after she had died of cancer. And anyway, everyone knew that office romances were not on the list of smart moves in life.

"You're right," she agreed with what Jesse had just said, absently brushing a crumb from her skirt. "People do have a tendency to resist change. And here- " Her voice trailed off, the thought left unspoken as she looked up at him.

"And here," Jesse finished the thought for her. "They don't trust anything they're not familiar with."

Finished with his lunch, Jesse was leaning back casually on the bench beside her. "Which is common in small towns. And in some cases, it's not going too far to term small towns as isolated societies."

Jesse was right. When Jenna had moved to Alder Grove five years ago, she had expected small-town charm, the whole idealistic Mayberry existence. And by all outward appearances Alder Grove was a quiet, peaceful little town. Slow-paced and laid back. A place here everyone waved to each other and ice cream socials were well attended.

But she had soon found that the people of Alder Grove tended to be closed-minded, judgmental and more than a little suspicious of anything or anyone new or different. They were especially mistrustful of outsiders. And Jenna and Jesse both fell into the category of outsiders. While Jesse had come from Chicago, she had grown up in the northern part of the state, in a moderate-sized town just a few miles south of the Wisconsin border.

"People are going to have a hard time accepting the idea that there might be a killer among them," Jenna said as she watched the children playing with the dog. "There isn't much crime to speak of around here. There never has been."

"Because for the most part everyone follows the rules," Jesse said without looking at her. He was also watching the dog. He lifted one dark eyebrow and said, "At least on the surface. Some communities stay so locked in a set pattern that they seem permanently frozen that way. Things stay the same. At all costs. Ideas, behaviors, beliefs, all those things get passed down from generation to generation. People are comfortable with what they know. They become so used to the familiar that they are afraid of anything that might jar the current order of things.

"It's the perfect breeding ground for this sort of thing though," he said. "You can keep some of the good things going, but, unfortunately, in some cases, you also have the potential for perpetuating some of the darker sides of human nature. Nothing is brought out into the open. Everyone is afraid to have the system shaken, even if it may be a harmful or destructive system." He looked at her. "You're right. This is definitely going to shake things up."

Jenna watched as he got up to toss both of their empty lunch bags into the nearest trash can.

"Most small towns have never had to deal with a murder," Jesse went on when he sat back down. "Let alone a series of murders. They just don't have the means to handle this kind of investigation. It's going to be critical that all the evidence is handled properly so that it can be admitted into court. Things can go wrong. Evidence can be mishandled, which can result in killers walking away free. I've seen it happen before.

"Of course," Jesse said after breathing a deep sigh and looking at her again. "There is a chance that I'm wrong about this."

A slight breeze ruffled a page of the magazine on the bench between them.

"But you don't think that you are," Jenna said quietly.

"No, I don't think that I am," Jesse replied with a slow shake of his head.

"How used to dealing with these kinds of things are you?" she asked.

"More used to it than I would like to be" he answered soberly.

"How do you deal with it?" she wanted to know. "I mean, you must have seen some terrible things over the years working as a homicide detective."

He was thoughtful for a few moments, one hand reaching to still the fluttering pages of the magazine. "I have. And you try, but you don't always deal well with it. Sometimes it is hard to maintain your professional detachment. There are things that you lose sleep over, things that haunt you. But you get angry, too, and you realize that someone has to be a voice for the victims because there is no one else to speak for them. And you don't want to see more victims."

One corner of his mouth drew back silent contemplation, which accentuated the groove in his cheek. "That. And experience helps."

"So what got you started in this line of work?" Jenna asked, watching him as she reached up to push a stray curl back behind her ear.

"I had an uncle who was a detective. When I was a kid, I thought he knew everything there was to know in the world. I wanted to be just like him. And then when he gave me my first chemistry set for Christmas, I was hooked. Of course, my mother didn't always appreciate my enthusiasm. Especially after I almost blew up her kitchen with my first volcanoes. I did impress my uncle though," he said with a soft chuckle.

"Volcanoes?" Jenna repeated with a questioning smile. "As in more than one?"

"I wanted more than the usual display, so I built a series of volcanoes rising out of my version of the ocean. And then I put together a pretty mean mixture of chemicals because I wanted extra powerful eruptions. They were extra powerful all right. The neighbors thought so. So did the fire department."

Jenna continued to watch him, bemused by the lingering smile on his face. The breeze touched silky strands of his ebony hair before he lifted one hand and pushed them back.

Jesse was a good-looking man. An incredibly good-looking man. His face was lean and sculpted with strong masculine lines that hinted at Native American blood somewhere in his ancestry. The ghost of a smile, still there, was especially potent. *If* she was vulnerable to such things. Which she was not. Still, she was honest enough with herself to admit that Jesse was handsome enough to be distracting at times.

"They're predicting nice weather for the next three days or so," he said, changing the subject. "Busy weekend planned?"

"I still have some packing to do," she replied. "A few more closets and drawers to empty. I'll have to remember to pick up some more boxes after work."

Jesse nodded slowly, noting the rainbow-like variations of color in the soft, honey-colored curls that fell over her shoulder before shifting his gaze to the branches above them. He focused on a squirrel that sat flicking its tail back and forth as it stared down at them.

Tilting his dark head back to watch the squirrel, which was now making its way along one of the electrical wires overhead, Jesse asked, "Why don't you come over for dinner Friday night? The kids have a movie night planned. I would take everyone out to a movie, but Abby doesn't do movie theaters very well. They're a little intimidating for her."

"That doesn't surprise me," Jenna remarked as she, too, lifted her face to watch the squirrel. Abby, who was nine years old, was a high-functioning autistic child.

"Hard to believe," Jesse said. "But around all the extra hours I'll be putting in at the office, Friday is still free. Other than that, I have a weekend of repairs to do around the house, a basketball game with Josh on Saturday morning, and Abby's first horseback riding lesson in the afternoon on Sunday."

He narrowed his gaze at the squirrel, which was peering down at them from the leaves above. The shadow of a smile touched his face. "Abby is excited about the lessons, but I'll probably have to drag her kicking and screaming at the last minute because it will be something new for her. Which has been known to spark a meltdown. But it does her more good to face her fears."

"How is Abby doing?"

"She misses her mother a lot. It's been rough on her. On Josh, too. But we take it one day at a time and somehow they are managing to cope." He paused and looked at her. "If you would like to come over, it would be good for Abby. She likes spending time with you. Josh likes you, too. You have a positive effect on both of them."

He graced her with another smile. "So, if you would like to come, Jenna, I can offer you a home-cooked meal and a movie. And I promise the movie won't have anything to do with serial killers."

"All right," Jenna relied. "Dinner and a movie do sound nice. Especially since almost everything I have to cook with has been packed away. I'll bring dessert. I'll have to surprise you, though, because I have no idea what I will bring."

"That's good," he said. "Because I have no idea what I will be cooking."

Chapter 3

Jesse leaned forward and opened the file on the desk before him. He carefully scanned the reports he had just received that morning. The Alder Grove Police Department didn't have the means to conduct the necessary forensic tests using the latest technology nor was an in-depth autopsy possible. But Springfield had one of the best crime labs in the state and the first test results had just come back.

All the blanks had been filled in. Jana Calder – Cause of Death: multiple stab wounds. Eleven to be precise. A prolonged and violent death condensed down to a few sheets of clinical terminology neatly stored in a manila envelope that would eventually be filed away on a shelf somewhere and forgotten. Except by the people she left behind. They would never forget. His eyes narrowed as he read the details further down the first page.

There was a notation made that Jana Calder had had pierced ears. It was further noted that there had been a deep tear on the left earlobe which had been hidden by the victim's hair. The report went on to describe in detail how the hair strands on that side had been matted down with mud and blood. It appeared, the report stated, that an earring had been torn violently from the earlobe.

No earring had been found at the crime scene. But it wasn't unusual for a killer to want to keep something that belonged to his victim. Personal objects were often kept as mementos or souvenirs. It could be anything. Jewelry, driver's licenses, articles of clothing. Jesse read on.

A small section of hair, about an inch in diameter, had been cut from the back of the young woman's head. Jesse didn't have to compare files. He already knew that Calia Devoss had had a similar lock of her hair cut off as well. Yeah, the perp was enjoying the game so much that he was collecting souvenirs.

The report also confirmed that Jana Calder had been sexually assaulted sometime before her death. He set aside the first page and began to read over the second. So far nothing stood out that might specifically point to the killer. Those traces of gravel found on the body turned out to be a mixture of mortar and gravel. They were doing further tests on it. No clear fingerprints had been lifted. No surprise there.

Contusions and bruises along the right side of the victim's body were consistent with a fall down a flight of stairs. The fall had occurred sometime before death. Her shoulder, though not dislocated, had been badly wrenched. Jesse had looked at enough autopsy reports to know that it would have been painful to move the shoulder, especially agonizing to be suspended from a tree. His mouth thinned grimly. Jana Calder had suffered a great deal, and the killer had loved every minute of it.

The third page contained the results of the tests on hair and fibers removed from the victim's clothing. Rope fibers. Common manila rope. Bits of tree bark were found over the victim's entire body. They were in her hair and embedded in the skin of her wrists. The bark was identified as oak. Specifically, white oak.

The results confirmed the theory that the victim had been suspended from a tree by her bound wrists which had extensive bruising and lacerations in a tell-tale circular pattern.

One thing could be deduced. The killer knew how to tie a specialized knot. The weight of the victim would have eventually worked a common knot loose.

The use of restraints was all about keeping his victims right where he wanted them. Sexual release was obviously one of the killer's goals. Arousal, possibly, also depending on the helplessness and the suffering of his victims.

In murders of this type, a pattern eventually emerged. Predictability was a key factor in finding and stopping a serial killer. If you could get into the mind of the killer and anticipate his behavior, you stood a better chance of stopping him. It wasn't a comfortable place to be, but years of training and experience had given Jesse a kind of instinct that he had learned to rely on when instinct was all there was to go on.

Also important was finding out how the killer chose his victims or where they were killed. Repeat killers were often compulsive in their patters. He knew of one murderer who killed only when the moon was full. Another had things carefully timed from the point of stalking, or hunting, so that he killed only on the eleventh day of each month. Jesse had Jenna checking weather reports, moon cycles and a long list of similar things.

And the killer himself? Early in life he almost certainly experienced trauma in the form of emotional, physical or sexual abuse, or all three, which damaged normal social development. Such events, or a series of them, could have a lasting impact on an individual. The normal nurturing relationship with his primary caretakers got twisted somehow. And somewhere along the line, during some critical period of learning, he would have identified with the wrong kind of role model, his own identity getting lost somewhere in the dark world of abuse. Jesse held firmly to the theory that killers were made, not born.

There might be a traceable history of violence or other antisocial behaviors early in the perpetrator's life. And maybe not. But recorded or not, for anyone looking, there would have been definite signs of a disturbed childhood. Antisocial tendencies, bizarre sexual activity, bullying or destructive behavior, the torture or killing of animals, these were often indicators of trouble later on in life.

Of course, that didn't necessarily mean there was a trail to follow. Isolation was also nearly always a factor that needed to be added into the equation. Families with deeply-rooted problems almost invariably kept to themselves and rarely reported such things. As a rule, they lived under the cover of secrecy. They had to if the dysfunctional system was going to thrive.

Unfortunately, murderers were also capable of keeping a perfectly normal front between themselves and the rest of the world. Many of them were described as charming, friendly and all-around good guys, which made identifying and catching them that much harder.

Jesse knew what he was up against. He had been a homicide detective for nine years. He was a stranger in Alder Grove. It wasn't going to be easy to get people to open up to him.

What was even more troubling was that the bodies of both women had been found by accident. Calia Devoss' body had been found in an abandoned root cellar only by chance. Jana Calder had been buried in a shallow grave near a cemetery, the remains discovered only after a hunting dog had begun to dig her up.

The killer was taking pains to hide the bodies of his victims and if it hadn't been for accidental discoveries, they would still be hidden. The question was, were there other victims that hadn't yet been found?

He scanned the fine print of the paper before him. He sat frowning at a separate notation that had been hand written beside a typed paragraph. An earring had been found in the victim's pocket. The earring was small but it was being checked for prints. The results weren't in yet.

Jesse flipped back through the pages in the file. Was the earring found in the right or the left pocket? The right. That was not the same side as the earlobe with the deep scratch. Had the earring simply been lost, or had it been hidden from the killer, he wondered. He had no way of knowing. Not at the moment. But somewhere along the line it might prove to be a valuable bit of information.

And then he came across another page of the autopsy report. It was at the back of the folder and had been filed out of order. Looking it over, he leaned back in his chair as he re-read the final findings in the report.

There was a substantial amount of blood on the right forefinger which had collected under the fingernail. And further down, he read: One of the deceased's ribs had been removed.

The muscles about Jesse's mouth tightened into grim lines. He knew what those things meant. And he knew, too, that mutilation was always likely to progress. For now there was no way of knowing when the killer would resume the hunt. But Jesse had no doubt, resume it he would.

He sat for a while, thinking over all he had just read. "So, Jana Calder," he said out loud. "Just what is it you were trying to tell us?"

This wasn't something he expected to encounter in Alder Grove. But he also knew that big cities didn't have a monopoly on serial killers. He looked up when Sheriff Wade walked into the office.

"I've just had a phone conversation with Orin Rath, a deputy over in Grant County," the sheriff informed him. "He's got something that may be related to our cases. A local girl was reported missing some time ago. It was treated as a runaway by the sheriff there, but Orin always thought there was more to it. I think it would be a good idea if you went up there and talked to the girl's family and see what you can piece together."

"I agree, Dell," Jesse said. He thought it would be a very good idea.

Chapter 4

Thunder rumbled like an angry beast growling out a prolonged warning. Lightning pulsed behind the black cloud mass that had pushed rapidly up from the horizon. It would rain, and soon by the looks of the sky.

Jenna went up the steps to the front porch. The house was showing unmistakable signs of age. There was paint peeling off the porch columns and both the ceiling and the floorboards of the porch needed repairs. The clapboard siding was faded except where shutters that had once flanked the two front windows had been removed.

But the house was not without its charm. Rose vines covered a trellis at one end of the porch, and here was a swing with a rose-patterned cushion. There were window boxes filled with newly-emerging seedlings and a ruby-colored hummingbird feeder hanging in one corner.

Jenna lifted her hand, about to knock when the front door suddenly swung open.

"Hi."

"Am I early?" Jenna asked, a little flustered.

Jesse stood in the front hallway, working at the buttons of his shirt. His bare chest showed in the opening. His very male, very bare chest. A chest she had never seen before.

"No," he replied in a slightly husky voice, a little flustered himself. "You're not early. I'm running late."

He must have just taken a shower because his dark hair was still damp where it curled over his collar.

"Come in." He swept a hand out and stood aside as he continued to work at the buttons.

Jenna had never been inside Jesse's home before. It was an old house with a wide staircase at the end of the foyer and dark, ornate trim everywhere. A doorway to her left opened to a spacious living room which was decorated, in part, with a Native American theme.

There were boldly-patterned rugs covering the hardwood floors and richly-colored tapestries on the walls. The pillows on the leather sofa had similar designs. The same theme was evident in the hand-thrown pottery that adorned the twin book shelves that flanked a massive stone fireplace.

"I'm sorry," Jesse apologized. "I got back late. There's a lot of ground to cover up there."

That morning, Jesse had gone back to the crime scene with a metal detector and a couple of deputies, looking for any evidence that might have been overlooked. They hadn't come up with anything, but with rain in the forecast, Jesse had wanted to check the surrounding woods before the storm. He had also made last-minute arrangements to talk to the parents of a missing girl up in Grant County. Tonight. Which meant that their movie and dinner plans had changed.

He looked at the foil-covered dish that Jenna was holding. "Here, let me take that from you. It must be dessert."

"Yes," she said as she handed the dish over. "It's pie."

"Pie?" he echoed, a wistful quality creeping into his voice. "What kind?"

"Peach."

"Did I tell you that peach was my favorite?"

"No," Jenna replied. "But when I saw you buy some peaches at the farmer's market after work last week, I assumed you liked them."

"You assumed right. Come on back to the kitchen."

Jesse set the pie on the counter. "There's a casserole in the oven- " he glanced at the clock. "Which is probably about ready," he said as he grabbed a dish towel and pulled the oven door open.

"Yeah, this is done." He lifted the casserole from the oven. "Gussie Hester made it earlier. She's a good cook, makes a mean chicken casserole." He set the casserole on a hot pad on the table.

"I started a salad earlier," he said. "There are tomatoes and cucumbers hiding somewhere in the vegetable drawer." He nodded towards the refrigerator. "If you wouldn't mind taking over, I'll finish getting dressed," he said as he tucked the tails of his shirt into his pants.

He whipped a tie out of his back pocket and drew it around his neck. "You know," he said as he worked with the tie. "This isn't exactly what I meant when I invited you over for dinner."

She was searching through the vegetable draw in the refrigerator. Finding a tomato, she said over her shoulder, "I'm glad to do it Jesse. I didn't have anything else to do tonight."

She dug out a cucumber and brought the vegetables to the table. Jesse opened a drawer and handed her a knife.

"The kids have to be in bed no later than 11:00," Jesse was saying as she sliced into the tomato. "They know the deal. They get to watch a movie only after they have finished their homework."

Jenna had always been impressed by Jesse's patient way with both of the children. She knew it couldn't be easy for him. He had his hands full being a full-time parent, a job that had been suddenly thrust upon him almost overnight.

"Make sure they do the dishes," Jesse said as he flexed his wrist into a watch. "Does this tie look straight?"

The tie was straight, and a good thing, too. No way did she want to get close enough to adjust it for him.

They both turned to look at the window as the first heavy drops of rain struck the glass. Lightning zigzagged across the dark sky. Thunder rumbled in its wake.

"I'll probably be late." He didn't add the 'Don't wait up for me.' part, but although she had been married before, this was as close to a domestic scene as Jenna had ever gotten.

"That's all right," she said. "Just be careful driving in the rain. The weather channel predicted possible tornadoes. And flooding."

"I saw that, too. Thanks, Jenna," Jesse said as he grabbed his wallet and car keys off the counter. "I'll make this up to you."

Through windows streaming with rain, Jenna stood for a few moments watching the headlights of Jesse's car as it pulled out of the driveway. It was bad weather for a long drive, and it was supposed to keep up all night. She turned back to the table and picked up the knife.

This was nice, she thought as the tomato pieces joined the cucumber and lettuce in the bowl. Preparing a family dinner in Jesse's kitchen, and having someone to share it with while the rain was pouring down outside, gave her a surprisingly warm, cozy feeling inside.

She had forgotten how relaxing sharing a meal and some pleasant conversation around a dinner table could be. It had been a long time

26

since she had shared an evening with anyone. Even with her ex-husband, Kane, there had never been much conversation at mealtimes. When he actually took the time to eat with her, which hadn't been very often.

But she didn't want to think about Kane tonight, she thought as she dried her hands on a dish towel. She finished setting the table, then called Josh and Abby down to eat.

It had been a long drive up here in the pouring rain and it was going to be a long drive back to Alder Grove. Jesse hadn't eaten since breakfast and he was looking forward to some of Gussie's chicken casserole and a generous piece of Jenna's peach pie when he got back home.

He hadn't expected this interview to be a pleasant social call, but he also hadn't anticipated that he would have to remind himself more than once to maintain his professional detachment.

The girl's name was Keara Eland. She had been sixteen when she disappeared. Missing for almost a month now, she would have turned seventeen just two days ago. There was a group of pictures of Keara on a small table beside the sofa. One was a candid photograph where she had turned and was caught laughing by the person taking the picture. There were also several pictures of a younger Keara and one taken together with her mother.

Jesse jotted down another note and asked, "And your daughter didn't leave a note behind?"

The mother shook her head. "No."

"Did Keara ever run away before?"

Again the mother shook her head, but this time she looked like she wanted to say something more. With downcast yes, she repeated her previous answer.

The woman kept opening and closing her hands in her lap. "I heard about the m- " She had a hard time even saying the word. "The murders in Greene County. You're sure you don't have any information that you're not telling me?" she asked, her expression bleak as if she dreaded even the asking.

Jesse did his best to reassure her. "No, Mrs. Crayden. This is just a routine interview." He chose his words carefully. "We want to be as thorough as possible."

She nodded while her fingers plucked nervously at the buttons at the throat of her sweater. He knew this was difficult for her. The reports of the murder must have made her even more apprehensive about her daughter's safety.

"Was there any indication at all that Keara might be thinking about running away? Did she ever threaten to do so?"

"It was a big adjustment for Keara when we moved here," the woman said. "She did talk about running away."

"More than once?"

Another nod was the mother's reply.

"Would you say that your daughter's threats to run away were brought on by anything specific?" Jesse asked, again choosing his words carefully. "Or is it your opinion that it was the usual sort of teenage rebelling?"

"I- Yes, that. Rebelling."

Again, Jesse had the distinct impression that there was more here than what the woman was saying. Her voice was telling him that, and so was her body language.

The husband spoke up. "Celeste, why don't you go out to the shed and get me a sody?"

Jesse caught the momentary flash in the woman's eyes. He saw the stiffening of her back and the tightening of her jaw before she wordlessly rose from her chair and left the room.

Jesse had decided from the beginning that this interview would be more productive without the husband's presence. The man hadn't said much so far, but his silence itself was full of meaning.

Right away, there had been something about Ulfert Crayden that got under Jesse's skin. There was something bordering on sarcasm in the man's demeanor and in the subtle shifting of his posture. And he watched his wife like a hawk.

It hadn't taken long to figure out that Crayden was a domestic tyrant who demanded total obedience. He was lord of this rundown castle, ruler of his wife and family. Jesse had seen the type before. He ordered his wife around like a servant and thought that made him better than her.

The man sat sprawled back in a threadbare brown recliner that had seen better days. His well-fed belly strained against a stained and faded shirt. There was a can of chew on the table beside him and two empty beer cans, both crushed, lying beside the chew.

"And what was your relationship with Keara like, Mr. Crayden?"

Crayden let his breath out in a snort. "Fine. Considerin'."

"Can you elaborate?"

The man's eyes squinted suspiciously for a moment, as if he didn't trust anyone who used words not in his usual vocabulary.

"I can e-lab-or-ate," Crayden replied, dragging the word out. "The girl was wild. Always running around." The chair squeaked as he shifted his considerable weight to make himself more comfortable. "Tell you what you ought to be doing," he said. "You ought to be talking to them friends of hers."

"Keara had a lot of friends?"

"Did," came the reply followed by a deep belch. "I'll tell you how it was," the man went on confidentially. "Even though the girl wasn't my responsibility, I gave her a roof over her head and fed her."

And you think you deserve a medal for generosity? Jesse thought to himself.

"But the kid was trouble from the start," the stepfather went on.

"Keara, you mean?"

"Yeah," Crayden nodded. "And the kids she brought around here were trouble, too. I run 'em off. I run 'em all off. Kids traipsing through here all hours of the day and night." He let his breath out shortly. "Celeste made a mistake in babying her and letting her have her way all the time. The girl is probably sitting back right now," he added. "Laughing at all this attention she's getting."

"So you believe Keara ran away voluntarily?"

He nodded. "Like I said, I gave her a roof over her head and fed her. And she paid me back with a smart mouth.

"She had a friend. Named Felicia." Crayden drawled the name, not bothering to hide the leer on his face. He picked up a used toothpick from the table beside him and began to pick at a rotted tooth in the front of his mouth. "I expect that little heifer is hiding Keara somewheres."

"You think this friend may know where Keara is?"

"I'll bet she knows just where she is."

"What about this Felicia? Did you run her off, too, like you ran off the others?"

Jesse waited while Crayden dug at another tooth on the other side of his mouth. "Should have. That girl was ornery. I come across her and Keara swimming in the creek one day. By accident. They didn't-I didn't know they were there."

Sure, Jesse thought to himself.

"Well, this kid, she was a bad influence on Keara." Crayden leaned forward and became more animated. "Man to man," Which was a

29

matter of opinion, Jesse thought to himself. "The girl had tits out to here." Crayden held both hands out in front of his chest, as if he was relishing the memory. "Felicia was always teasing and flashing them tits around. If you know what I mean."

Jesse knew exactly what he meant and his fist itched to smash the leer off the man's face.

"Well, I listened to the little tramp braggin' about how many boys she'd had- "

"Felicia?"

"Yeah. It shocked the hell out of me. Kids today." He shook his head. "Don't seem to know where to draw the line." He snorted again, his eyes narrowing slyly. His features hardened as if at some unpleasant recollection.

Jesse's sixth sense, honed fine after years of interrogations, was filling in the blanks. He had the impression that Felicia had drawn the line where Ulfert Crayden was concerned and that he hadn't liked it. Jesse didn't have any proof, however, and Crayden sure wasn't going to admit it to him. But if the man was inappropriate towards his stepdaughter's underage friends, it was possible that he had been inappropriate with Keara as well. It was something to keep in mind.

Crayden pointed his toothpick at Jesse. "And something else about that little sneak Keara you should know. She's a damned thief. Had some money come up missing after she left."

"How much was missing?"

"About six hundred dollars. I noticed it a few days after Keara left."

"Do you usually keep big amounts of money like that lying around the house?"

"Yep."

"Did you report it?"

"Nope," Crayden answered shortly and then settled silently back in his chair when his wife came back and handed him a soda. She offered one to Jesse.

"No, thank you, Mrs. Crayden," Jesse said as he flipped his notebook closed.

"Are we through here?" Crayden wanted to know as he popped open his can of soda. He didn't waste any time tearing into his wife when the soda foamed all over his lap.

After the man's last profanity, Jesse informed him, "I think I have everything I need."

The rain had let up but it looked like it was going to start up again soon. Jesse paused in the driveway before getting into his car. Celeste Crayden had appeared from the side of the house. She looked pale and fragile in the brief flickers of lightning that lit her face. She stood there, not speaking, but hugging herself and hanging her head for long moments before she began in a shaky voice.

"Life was never easy for Keara," she said, looking up. "Her real father died when she was six. She's never really gotten over that. Then we moved here and- " She closed her eyes for a long time before she could go on. "And things just got worse. I know I didn't provide my daughter with the kind of home life she should have had. I tried, but things didn't work out the way I thought they would. I'm here- I'm only staying because Keara needs a place to come back to when she is ready to come home. I have to be here waiting for her. She has to know where to find me."

There was a kind of desperation in the woman's eyes and Jesse knew she was fighting the tears. She swallowed and went on after a quick glance towards the house. "I have a little money put aside and as soon as Keara is back- " Her voice broke.

"I understand," Jesse said quietly.

"Did he tell you that Keara stole money from him?" Bitterness had crept into her voice. "He's lying. It isn't true. He was jealous of my relationship with Keara. He would do or say anything to ruin that. Just like he would say or do anything to make Keara look bad. Even now."

"Have you discussed any of this with the local authorities?" Jesse wanted to know.

"The local sheriff is a friend of my husband. Thy hunt together. They fish together. I don't expect any help from him."

She caught her lower lip between her teeth. "There is more. Keara did leave a note. She'd had a fight with Ulfert the day she disappeared. He tore the note up and told me not to say anything to anyone about it. In the note Keara said that Ulfert had been drinking and abusive that day and that she couldn't live with him anymore. She said that he had told her that if she didn't like the way things were, she should leave. Keara wrote that she was going to do that, find somewhere else to live.

31

But she also said that she would call me and let me know she was all right." She closed her eyes tightly. Her lip quivered. "She never called.

"Keara is the only good thing that I have in my life. I want my little girl home. I just want her back." Her eyes were pleading now. "You are certain that you don't know anything more than what you have told me?"

"I don't have any information beyond that," Jesse assured the woman.

"You promise me you will tell me as soon as you hear anything?"

"I promise, Mrs. Crayden, if anything changes, I will let you know right away."

He reached two fingers into his shirt pocket and gave her his business card. "If you hear anything or think of something else, call me. If you need *anything*," he emphasized the word. "Call. I promise I will do everything I can to find your daughter."

Chapter 5

Jesse didn't flip the light switch on the wall beside the back door. He took his shoes off and, in the dim light of the kitchen, made his way quietly through the hallways to the thermostat and turned the heat up.

Except for the nightlight in the kitchen, the house was dark. Jenna was asleep on the couch and the kids, apparently, had obeyed their curfew. Soundless in his stockinged feet, he went back into the kitchen.

He had noticed a bottle of wine setting on the counter. Gussie Hester sometimes used wine for cooking. The bottle was less than half full, and not very potent stuff, but maybe it would take the edge off some. He picked up the bottle, retraced his steps and stood looking out the back door.

The rain was still pouring down. He flexed the muscles in both shoulders to ease the tension there and massaged the back of his neck with one hand. He didn't bother with a glass but lifted the bottle to his mouth and took a long drink.

Lightning blazed a forked trail down the sky. Dead white lightning that flickered like a strobe. It emphasized a sky blacker than the deepest corners of Hell. In the distance a lingering rumble of thunder rolled across the darkness.

No sense in waking Jenna. Since she was already asleep, she might as well spend the rest of the night rather than drive home in the pouring rain. He leaned his forearm on the door frame and continued to watch the rain outside.

He lifted the bottle again and drank deeply. Rubbing the back of his hand across his beard-stubbled chin, he drew a long breath and released it in a sigh. He was having a hard time shaking his mood tonight. There was something about rainy nights like this that made it easy for a man to get lost in his darker thoughts.

He finished the last of the wine in the bottle while his dark brows settled into a frown. The image of Keara Eland from the photographs, laughing and full of life, the innocence of childhood still lingering her eyes, blurred together with the image of her mother. He thought, too, of Jana Calder's mother and how she must be feeling tonight. How would he cope if it was Abby? He couldn't imagine.

He couldn't forget the look on Celeste Crayden's face. He kept hearing the anguished pleading in her voice. Not knowing was always the worst part. It was like being caught in the middle of a nightmare and waiting for it to end. Hoping for resolution, but fearing it, too.

He narrowed his gaze at the shimmering curtain of rain. It looked like silver against the intense blackness of the sky. While the mother of one missing daughter prayed for her safe return tonight, the mother of another grieved for the child she would never see again. These kinds of murders, particularly, were often a death sentence for the survivors, too. The ones who had to go on.

He had seen things over the years that would never leave him. And it was true what he had said to Jenna. There were things that he lost sleep over. Things that could make a man believe in the existence of pure, unholy evil. Soul-sickening times when you came to the point of hoping the missing were already dead rather than still alive in the hands of that evil.

Keara Eland was out there somewhere on this rainy night. Maybe she was safe. He prayed she was simply a runaway. It was possible. But there was also a predator out there who was preying on girls like her. And he was taking advantage of his knowledge of miles and miles of remote wilderness to hide the evidence of his sick appetites. He knew about abandoned root cellars. No doubt he also knew about forgotten wells where a body could be hidden forever.

Put it out of your mind, he told himself. He had to be careful to keep himself at an emotional distance as much as possible. That was the only way he could do his job. He forced himself to think about all he had to do over the weekend. The basketball game with Josh. The riding lessons with Abby. And Jenna would be here for breakfast. Those were things he was looking forward to.

In a little bit the wine would ease the tension in him. And after it had mellowed him out some, he would get a bite to eat. By then he would be tired enough to fall asleep. Hopefully.

He went to the fridge, pulled out the casserole and spooned some chicken and rice onto a plate. He put the food into the microwave and set the timer. While he waited, he wandered to the living room and stood for a moment with one shoulder propped against the door frame.

His mother had taught him a great deal about his heritage. From her own mother she had learned about the old ways. Tonight he yearned for her wisdom and her understanding. She would know what to say to him to help him deal with the demons that were plaguing him.

Life is a circle, his mother had told him, one that leads back to the beginning. At the beginning is always the truth. What you end up with depends on which course you choose along the way. The circle begins and ends with your choices.

"The storm," he could almost hear her saying. "Listen to its song, Jesse. It will speak to you if you listen with your heart."

He closed his eyes. He missed her. And Laney. His sister's memory was alive in this house. It was alive in his heart, too. Josh and Abby were a part of who she had been. A circle, his mother would have said.

He watched Jenna sleeping. The faint light spilling from the kitchen lit the gold in her hair. As if she felt his scrutiny, she drew a deep breath. She stirred, opened her eyes and looked straight at him.

"You awake? he asked in a low voice.

Nodding, she put one hand over her mouth and yawned. "Is it still raining?" she asked sleepily.

"It is. You might as well stay dry and warm here and go home in the morning. It's still pouring down pretty hard."

After a moment's silence he said, "You can sleep in the guest room if the couch in uncomfortable."

She must have decided to stay. "This is fine," she said as she snuggled deeper under the blanket. "It feels like the temperature has drooped."

"It has. I just turned the heat up."

"Did it rain all the way up to your interview?"

"All the way there and back," he replied.

"I was a little worried. The TV said that the creek was out of its banks and that four inches of rain had fallen in an hour."

"I can believe that," he said, nodding.

35

"How did things go?" she asked, sitting up and yawning again.

"About the way these things usually go," he said. "There are a lot of unanswered questions."

The sound of rain drumming on the roof filled the silence.

"What time is it?" she asked.

"A little after midnight."

The microwave timer went off in the kitchen.

"There's enough food if you want to join me," he said.

"All right," Jenna said as the inviting aroma of the casserole filled the air. "You're right. Gussie Hester does make a mean chicken casserole. I wouldn't mind seconds."

He got two plates down from the cabinet. "So what movie did you end up watching?" he asked as he pulled the silverware drawer open.

"Pirates of the Caribbean," she answered. "Part Two."

He nodded. "One of Abby's favorites."

She sat down at the table and rubbed her bare toes.

"Feet cold?" he asked.

"A little."

He went to the back porch and returned with a laundry basket. He set it on the floor between them and started to dig through it.

"Sock basket," he explained. He held up a purple sock. Matching socks have a habit of disappearing around here." He leaned over, digging deeper into the overflowing basket.

Jenna watched Jesse's downbent head. She had always been aware of depth in Jesse's eyes. And intelligence. But tonight she saw something more. Tonight she could see the strain etched in his features. She could sense a tension that he was trying to keep to himself.

His tie was undone. His sleeves were rolled back revealing muscular forearms. The effect of the low light on ebony hair held her gaze while the shadow of a beard accentuated his maleness and gave him a roguish, almost piratical look. Her imagination was working overtime, she told herself. No doubt because she had just finished watching a movie about pirates.

He looked up at her. "It's one of the great mysteries of the house." He smiled and his face changed, lost some of its hardness. "Where all the matching socks go."

He straightened holding up another purple sock that matched the first one and handed it to her.

"That was easy. These are Abby's. She likes these soft, fluffy socks."

"I like them, too," Jenna said, wiggling her toes in the soft purple socks.

Jesse put the laundry basket away, then grabbed a hot pad and opened the microwave door.

"Do you want some salad?" Jenna asked while he brought the steaming dish to the table.

"Sure," he said.

She brought the salad bowl to the table along with some dressing. "I don't know if I've ever met a man who actually ate salads."

"No?" Jesse lifted one dark brow in her direction.

"No. My ex-husband thought he was too macho to eat anything that didn't have grease or blood oozing out of it. Fruits and vegetables were definitely not on his menu. Like most of the people around here, hunting and fishing were a big part of his upbringing. They ate what they caught."

"I guess that makes me *un*macho," Jesse said as he spooned some salad onto his plate. "The only hunting I ever did was for a good steak at the supermarket. And we grew up having fruits and vegetables with all our meals, mostly from my mother's garden."

"Do you like to cook?" she asked.

"Actually I do," he said. "It used to be hard sometimes to justify cooking an entire meal for just one person. But now- " He shrugged wide shoulders. "The kids need to learn to eat healthy foods. And I think that family meals are important, so I try to stick to a routine whenever I can."

She had to admire Jesse. It was clear to her that he was making every effort to make the best home life possible for the two children whose lives had been shaken first by a divorce and then by the loss of their mother.

"Is there any pie left?" He got up from the table and lifted one corner of the foil covering the dish.

"This is a *homemade* peach pie," he said as he brought the pie to the table.

"Yes. I bought the peaches at the farmer's market yesterday."

"I haven't had a homemade pie in years," he said. "I hate to think of how long it's been."

Jenna watched Jesse transfer a generous piece of pie to his plate. She didn't think there was a woman alive who would call Jesse unmacho. Suddenly the image of his bare chest flashed into her mind. That hard-muscled, bare chest with the thin line of dark hair trailing down the center of his flat, washboard belly and disappearing into the waistband of his pants seemed to be etched permanently into her brain.

She frowned and did her best to dislodge the image. She liked Jesse. Very much. Their relationship, however, was based on friendship. Friendship was uncomplicated. Friendship was safe.

She didn't want to even think about having a man in her life. Not in the foreseeable future at least. As soon as her divorce had been final, before the ink was barely dry on the paper, she had been surprised at how many men had come out of the woodwork wanting to date her. She had refused every one of them. There was, she had found, too much freedom given up in a relationship. Too much sacrifice.

Still this intimate sharing of food and conversation at the end of the day was what she had always imagined marriage should be. Both of them sitting here in stockinged feet together at midnight gave her a surprisingly warm feeling. It was a facet of domestic life she had missed out on, this sharing of quiet confidences. Or sharing of anything for that matter.

"Did you like the movie?" he asked her.

"Yes, and the card games afterwards."

"You beat them I hope" he said, looking up. "Because when they play cards with me, they're ruthless."

"Well, actually I did."

He smiled. A very slow, very sexy smile.

She looked down at her plate and made herself ignore the smile. She had enjoyed the movie. And she had enjoyed playing cards afterwards. She had also had time to study the living room as they had played.

The room had a bold, masculine look to it. But there was warmth there, too. It was an inviting, comfortable room. She had read the titles of some of the books on the shelves. There was a shelf dedicated to psychology, forensics and child rearing. Another shelf held poetry and nature books alongside some classics. Other titles were about Native Americans.

The wall hangings were exquisitely woven with vibrant colors and patterns. The artwork around the room was very good, very expressive. Above the fireplace was a watercolor painting of a Native American warrior on a horse. She had studied the picture earlier, impressed by the bold passion that had inspired the artist and his, or her, talent and ability to express that passion.

There were also several groupings of framed photographs. These filled three entire shelves. She recognized Josh and Abby in many of the pictures, taken at different ages. A pretty, dark-haired woman that Jenna knew as their mother smiled back at her from some of the photos.

There were several pictures of Jesse with his sister, more than one taken when they were children. There was a large photograph of a younger, shirtless Jesse riding a long-maned, half wild-looking black horse.

Again her thoughts drifted. She imagined Jesse shirtless at the end of the day, relaxed and waiting for her. Smiling . . .

What was wrong with her? This wasn't like her. These wayward imaginings belonged to giddy schoolgirls, not mature adult women who happened to be having an innocent meal with their co-worker.

Still, she tried to assure herself that it was perfectly normal to have such thoughts. Jesse was a good-looking man. A very good-looking man. The situation that they were in was almost intimate and a stray moment or two of fantasy was to be expected. Wasn't it? As long as Jesse never suspected the direction her thoughts were taking, there was no harm done.

She looked at him blankly, realizing he had just said something to her. One corner of his mouth was tilted upward in a smile.

"You went somewhere on me." Still smiling, he repeated what he had said. "What I said was that was the best peach pie I ever had."

"Thank you," she said, a little flustered at the compliment. She wasn't used to compliments about her cooking. In fact, she had gotten used to criticisms. About her cooking, her cleaning, her appearance and anything else her ex-husband could find to complain about.

"I'm glad you liked it. And I like your house, especially your living room" she said. "Did you decorate it?"

"Partly," he replied. "Laney had some pieces of furniture that had been passed down in the family. I combined hers with mine when I moved in here. I didn't want to change things too much because the kids had been through so many changes already. Change can be especially hard for Abby. Laney did the tapestries. It was one of her hobbies."

"They're beautiful. And the sketch over the fireplace, was that yours? Or hers?"

"In a way, it was both of ours," Jesse replied. "Laney had gotten the idea for it. I had more time for artwork back then. I painted it for her as a birthday present a few years ago."

"You are the artist?" Jenna asked, surprised.

He nodded.

"You're very talented."

He shrugged. "I've sold a few pieces over the years. But I don't have much time for it any more."

"Would you like to have more time for it?"

He nodded slowly. "Yeah. Sometimes I miss it."

Jesse was full of surprises, Jenna thought to herself. She'd had no idea he was such an accomplished artist.

"Right now we keep busy working on this house," he was saying. "We did some re-modeling in the kitchen. Re-siding is our next venture. This house is nearly a hundred years old and it needs a lot of work. But it's well built," he went on. "My sister's ex-husband didn't lift a finger to repair or improve anything when he lived here. Laney did what she could, but when she got sick, she wasn't up to doing much work herself. And she wanted to spend what time she had with her kids."

Jenna nodded. She would have felt the same way herself.

"Without a husband to help her out, it was rough," Jesse went on. "Shortly after her diagnosis, Bryce left her for another woman. They all had to adjust to that, too."

"How terrible," Jenna murmured sympathetically. "I can't imagine a man turning his back on his family at a time like that."

"I'll admit, Bryce Edmonds isn't one of my favorite people," Jesse said. "But then Bryce always thought about himself first."

"Does he have anything at all to do with his children?" Jenna asked.

"No."

"I don't understand how a man could abandon his children like that."

"Believe me," Jesse said soberly. "He did them a favor."

"He was that bad?"

"That bad."

"Raising children with two parents is hard, Jesse. This has to be a huge adjustment for you."

He sighed deeply. "I won't say that it hasn't been that. Sometimes I wonder if they would be better off in a more traditional family setting, an environment with more structure and stability than I can offer them. I don't have much experience with parenting. In fact, I don't have any. And Abby needs so much attention that I worry about how she is going to cope with things as she gets older. Kids with autism don't handle change very well. Abby has had to deal with the loss of her mother along with everything else. She has some rough days."

"You are lucky Gussie Hester is so good with her."

"Yes, we were lucky there," Jesse agreed. "I would hate to think about what would happen if Abby didn't like the woman. But Gussie has a way with her. She's almost like the grandmother that Abby never had. In spite of the autism, Ab's a very strong-willed child." He lifted a dark brow in her direction. "We have days when all hell breaks loose. I have some background in my training to deal with it, and I keep trying to learn all I can. But it's not always easy.

"One thing is certain," he went on. "If I don't keep them, Bryce could step into the picture. And I'm not about to let that happen. I promised Laney that I wouldn't let him get his hands on them. I intend to keep that promise."

How different men were from one another, Jenna thought. Jesse was kind and thoughtful. And patient. He was also a man of integrity and responsibility. He kept his promises.

"Laney realized that she had made a mistake marrying Bryce," Jesse said. "But she couldn't have foreseen that. People don't always reveal who they really are in the beginning. Bad marriages happen."

"Yes," Jenna agreed. "Unfortunately, they do."

She had never talked much about her own failed marriage or her ex-husband with Jesse and he had never pried into her personal life. Even though Jesse's deep understanding of psychology made him more knowledgeable than most men, she had preferred to leave those unpleasant memories behind her. At the moment, however, it seemed natural to open up to him.

"I certainly had no idea that my marriage was going to make me so completely miserable. At first, I thought we shared the same values and had the same goals. Kane certainly gave me that impression." She sighed deeply. "But my marriage was doomed even before it began," she said. "Kane was never able to get beyond his past. He couldn't make the emotional break from his original family."

"That had to be rough for you."

"It was a nightmare," she confessed. "The Blackwells are like a family of vampires. Driven by an obsessive need to cling together, they weren't about to let Kane live his own life. And Kane didn't seem to know where they ended and he began."

"It sounds like they were deeply enmeshed."

"Yes. But Kane let it happen. He even encouraged it in ways that I didn't see then, but I can see it very clearly now. He put more effort into building walls between us than building a marriage. Sometimes," she said. "Eventually, you have to acknowledge walls and that some of them are unscalable."

Jesse nodded. "I take it that it wasn't an easy break?"

She shook her head. "No. And Kane still comes around playing the old games and pressuring me to give the marriage another try."

"Is that something you would consider?" Jesse asked, watching her face closely. "Getting back together with him?"

"No. Absolutely not. I would never put myself through that again."

"Unfortunately," Jesse said. "There are a lot of dysfunctional families around."

"Yes," she agreed. "And the Blackwells are dysfunctional enough to have created a murderer in their midst."

"Really." Jesse looked at her, his curiosity piqued.

"Kane's brother, Nolan, was the oldest Blackwell brother. There were three of them. Nolan was murdered thirteen years ago. It caused quite a stir around here, as you can imagine. The cousin who committed the murder is still in jail for the crime. He lived with the family off and on during his childhood.

"There were seven children in all, if you count the cousins that were absorbed into the family because their mother, as I heard it, moved from man to man. When it was convenient for her, she left her children behind. At least that's the story as I have heard it. From all that I have been able to put together, there was a lot of animosity between the two groups of children."

"No surprise there," Jesse remarked as he leaned back in his chair. "It must have been a rough situation on everyone."

Jenna nodded. "The more you get to know the family, the more you get the feeling that the murder was just the tip of the iceberg. It's hard to know just what really did go on because they are all pretty secretive about everything. But there's something dark there. Something you can almost feel."

After a shrug, she said. "Well, if we could write the chapters, we would choose happily-ever-afters every time. Unfortunately, life doesn't work that way." She yawned and stretched.

Jesse glanced at the clock. "It's been a long day. We should get some sleep."

Half an hour after they had said good-night, Jesse was still awake in his room. Lying on his back, he stared up into the darkness. Thunder muttered sullenly in the distance, making him wonder if yet another storm was on the way.

He thought of Jenna lying on his couch, warm and sleep-tossled. He imagined her here beside him in the darkness of his room and admitted to himself that he would like nothing better than to put his arms around her and draw her warmth to him while the rain was pouring down outside.

And then that thought led to another and his thoughts wandered a little into the forbidden. He knew he shouldn't be thinking about Jenna this way. Not that there was anything wrong with a little fantasizing, especially as long as he had been without a woman. There just wasn't any room for anything like dating in his life.

Nothing wrong with a little fantasy, he assured himself again. It was just a healthy male reaction to a beautiful woman. As long as Jenna never knew about those fantasies, there was no harm done. There was one thing he did not want to do, and that was to ruin their friendship. It had come to mean too much to him.

Chapter 6

The fire spread deep inside him as he tilted the bottle and drank deeply. The dark, potent liquid was a comfort against the damp chill. Or at least it would be when it reached his blood stream. Lightning clawed another jagged line in a sky that was black as pitch. Thunder muttered a belated warning as he slowly wiped his mouth with the back of his hand.

During its split-second existence, the lightning had picked up gold glints from the label of the bottle he held in his hand. It revealed the water shimmering on his raincoat. He had kept the raincoat for many years. It cocooned him with a comforting sense of security, of familiarity, wrapping around him like the warmth of a wood stove, sheltering him, hiding even his face . . .

Slipping the bottle into one of the large pockets of the raincoat, he turned and went down the steep wooden steps. A match rasped. The tiny flame flared, was touched to a wick and a halo of golden light spread out into the darkness.

Shadows danced along the old stone walls writing like a distorted play of demonic revelry. Wooden beams dissected the small space. The smell of mildew and dampness pervaded the air, along with the acrid smell of heated kerosene. This was his place, secure and unviolated and completely isolated from the rest of the world.

He drew something out of his other pocket. He liked the way it sparkled, especially in the candlelight. He liked the reflection glinting off the small disk of gold cradled in his palm. This was his now, too. It belonged to him. Forever.

He had pulled it out of his pocket to admire it many times. He like looking at it. He was able to focus when he held it. It gave him a sense of having her near him. It helped him relive it all over again.

He wanted to relive it. He wanted to savor every intense, breathless moment. Remembering filled him with a sense of satisfaction so deep that he was drawn to it again and again. So deep that it warmed him more than the whiskey he had just consumed.

He closed his eyes now, recalling the look of fear in her eyes and the way she had begged for her life. And the look in those eyes when she had realized she was going to die. He especially like that. It was almost as good as how he had felt at the last moment, the very moment when he had seen the life go out of those eyes. Having the ultimate power of life and death had come as a heady revelation to him a long time ago. He had experimented for many years, but nothing could compare with extinguishing the life in human eyes.

He frowned suddenly as he stood there with the shadows wavering fitfully around him. He still didn't know where the other earring was. He had searched everywhere for it, but it had vanished as if into thin air. It preyed at his mind. It would continue to gnaw at him, he knew, like a plague of black flies on a dead body until he discovered its whereabouts.

Losing it was not good. Not good at all. He had always prided himself on his thoroughness. Thoroughness kept you safe. Thoroughness gave you an edge. Next time he would be more careful.

The frown that etched his features settled into a scowl. She had called him a loser. He had never like being called that. His eyes changed.

In this particular game he was always the winner. She had lost. Her life, bitch that she was. A pretty bitch, though, who had thought she was too good for him. He had seen that in her eyes, too.

And because of all he had seen in her eyes, she had deserved everything he had done to her. It was a fitting payback for all the rejection, and all the scorn, and the way she had dared to laugh at him in the beginning. She should have treated him better. She had learned that lesson in the end.

The longer he lived, the deeper the conviction that all women were the same. They hid their real thoughts and motives so that they could get what they wanted. And if you forgot that they were the enemy, if you were foolish enough to trust them, then there was always a price to pay.

He was too smart to fall into their traps. Too smart not to have learned from the past.

He put the earring back into his pocket, crossed the low-ceilinged space and pulled the journal from its hiding place. It slipped easily out of the deep crevice in the wall. He brushed away the crumbles of mortar along with a small black spider and opened the book. The pages fell open to the right place, the one he was looking for.

He ran his forefinger over the lock of tawny hair. It reminded him of anothers. He held it to his face for a moment, breathing in the faint trace of perfume it still contained.

He turned several pages, picked up a pen, and wrote:

Last night I dreamed of feeding off a woman. I drank her blood. I tasted it in my mouth. These dreams I have lately haunt me. They stay with me. It is as if there is some kind of living darkness woven through them. Dark like blood. This darkness is like a liquid oozing out over my soul and I can't wait for it to overcome me again because I make this better each time and I am anxious to let this lead me even deeper than before. I understand now. The life is in the blood . . .

He liked putting the words down on paper. It seemed that by doing so the words began to take on a life of their own.

After he had finished with his thoughts he carefully returned the book to its hiding place. Next time he would write in blood. How much more powerful the words would be then. He wondered that he had not thought of it before.

He then opened a long, intricately-painted tin box. Inside was his most prized possession. He picked up the polished bone, carried it to the light, sat down and began to carve the carefully-though-out design.

Jenna had awakened early in the morning to the sound of rain. It was late afternoon and the rain was still falling. The temperature had dropped by quite a few degrees. A cold wind was blowing and every now and then a strong gust of wind would rattle the windows.

The windows were old and loose and bare. She had taken all the curtains down and packed them away in boxes. She folded the last of the kitchen curtains and set them in the box on top of the others. She would drop them off at the Help Center next week. She had already bought new curtains because she wanted as few reminders of the past as was possible in her new house.

Her slippered feet made a soft whisper on the kitchen floor as she crossed the room. Other than that sound and the occasional gusts of the wind, the house gave back only silence. It always had. Marriage, she knew, should not be loneliness. But being in a bad relationship, she had discovered, was sometimes lonelier than actually being alone. In marriage, silence could be a killing thing. And this house had been like a tomb of silence.

It was days like this, however, that reminded her of new beginnings. She had spent the last few weeks emptying closets and packing boxes. Almost all the shelves and cabinets were empty. She was more than ready to move on. She had found a smaller house closer to town to rent which would be much easier to take care of. Maybe, eventually, she would leave Alder Grove altogether. She had considered it. She had no family here and Kane and his family had left only bad memories of his place.

She pulled the clip from her hair, sighing deeply as the weight of her long curls fell loose around her shoulders. She made herself a cup of hot tea, carried it to the living room and sat down on the sofa.

When she had first moved here, she had loved the quiet peace of the wilderness that surrounded the house. It had seemed like an idyllic haven to her. She had been looking for peace and quiet, and a new beginning. Maybe she had believed that Kane would fill the painful void left after her mother's death.

But she had lived a secluded life here with Kane and she had come to learn that it was the way he had planned it. This old farmhouse was only a few miles away from the family home where Kane had been raised as a boy. It was also only a few miles from the rest of his family and it had proven to be too close. It was just one more way that Kane remained attached to the past while she had remained an outsider.

Kane certainly was not an outsider. He would never leave Alder Grove. Like Bear Prichard, Kane had been born and raised here. He fit in perfectly, knew everyone, could tell you the local history and the lineage of practically every single person who lived in the entire county. And like most people around here, he was wary and suspicious of outsiders, clinging to what he knew and rejecting anything that even hinted at change. Which included her.

After working so hard at keeping her at a distance throughout their marriage, she found it ironic that he wanted them to get back together.

And he didn't like her moving away. He'd had plenty to say about that over the past few weeks. She had managed to avoid him these past three weeks, but she knew he would show up sooner or later. She knew Kane. She couldn't remember a time since she had known him when he didn't somehow try to disrupt her plans or her peace of mind.

Well, mostly she knew him. She hadn't thought he was capable of infidelity, especially so soon after the wedding. He had surprised her there. And if she hadn't gone through his truck that day, she might never have discovered his betrayal. So much for her family and friends congratulating her on what a great guy Kane was, or how lucky she was and how devoted he was to her. He had fooled her and everyone else.

She finished her tea, got up from the sofa and went back to packing. There was no sense in wasting any more time thinking about Kane or the past.

On the threshold of the living room she stopped dead in her tracks. Pivoting sharply, she locked the front door and then made sure all the windows were closed and locked as well. With all that was going on, she was definitely going to have to be more careful and change her habit of leaving everything unlocked.

She went into the kitchen and put together a potato salad and cole slaw for tomorrow. Jesse, along with Josh and Abby, had offed to help her move. They would be here first thing in the morning.

She stirred the homemade salsa that was simmering on the stove, replaced the lid and began to clean out the final cabinet, the one that held her spices.

The old house creaked and groaned from the fitful gusts of wind outside. Kane had always insisted that this house was haunted. More than once he claimed that he had heard the voices of the ghosts. It was an old house, but in all the time Jenna had lived here, she had never seen or heard anything resembling a ghost. She had never felt anything unusual and she had never been afraid here.

It was Kane's way of trying to keep her scared and dependent on him, she had decided. Maybe he thought she would ask him to move back in if he thought she was afraid to live alone. Only it wasn't going to work. Living alone was far more peaceful than living with Kane, ghosts or no ghosts. The only ghosts haunting Kane were from his past, she decided as she began packing the contents of her silverware drawer into an empty box.

When she was finished packing everything except for a few utensils she would need for dinner, she walked back into the living room. She opened the door to the front closet, took out one of Kane's winter coats that was still hanging there and removed it from the hanger. With the coat out of the way, she saw that she had overlooked a box at the back of the closet. She dragged the heavy box out into the living room and sat down with it at her feet.

The box contained some old photo albums and pictures that belonged to Kane. There were several large family albums and some loose pictures on top of them. She lifted one dusty album from the box and saw a heavy, gaudy wood frame in the box underneath it. She picked the frame up and held it up to the light and studied the old black and white photograph.

There were seven children standing in front of a big, white farmhouse. She recognized the house as Kane's boyhood home. The same house where the murder had taken place all those years ago.

The children were standing in the yard of the house in the dappled shade of a huge sycamore tree. In the background was Kane's father, dead now for four years. She recognized a much younger Kane standing beside his father. The father's arm was draped over Kane's shoulder, the large arm possessively gripping Kane's chest.

If the stories were true, and she had no reason to believe they weren't, Kane's father had been a strict disciplinarian who had wielded an iron hand over his wife and children. A brutal man, in her opinion, who had demanded obedience and devotion without question. A man so hard and callous that neighbors brought him unwanted dogs and cats that he would dispose of for them. A thing that Jenna found thoroughly repugnant.

There was a strong physical resemblance between father and son. The mouth was the same, although a hint of what she interpreted as aggressiveness was stronger in the father. At least in the photo. The eyes, full of mistrust and suspicion as they stared back at the camera, were similar. It was uncanny how much Kane looked like his father. It was as if he were cast in the very same mold, even down to the facial expression. There was the same forward thrust of the jaw. Very pronounced in the father, just beginning in the son.

The shape of the jaw, particularly, had been passed down strongly through the generations. In a very old, sepia-toned photograph that Jenna had once seen, a distant male relative had had the same square jaw line. So did Kane's other two brothers.

Even Kane's sister, Vidia, had similar bone structure. It made Vidia undeniably masculine looking. Not that Vidia seemed to mind. In all the years that Jenna had known Vidia, she had never seen the woman wear a speck of makeup or choose a flattering hairstyle that would have softened her features.

It was the same with her clothing. It was as if she wanted to look harsh, forbidding and unfeminine. If that were the case, Jenna thought, Vidia had certainly succeeded very well.

Jenna dug through the box and found another picture of Kane and his father. There was one with all three brothers standing together. The cousins were only in the one picture.

Jenna stared at the group picture, wondering which one of those children had been capable of murder. She turned the picture over. There were some faded dates written down but no names. No way of identifying who was who, she realized, as she put the pictures back in the box.

She picked up one of the albums to set it on to of the pictures when some loose pictures fell out of the pages. She gathered up the pictures and saw almost the identical scene on each one, only taken from a slightly different angle. These were not black and white pictures. They were in full, vivid, disturbing color.

Kane's brother, Randal's, hunting pictures, she thought with distaste. Yes, there was Randal Blackwell in one of the pictures, proudly posing with his rifle beside his trophy, a gutted deer hanging from a tree, the ground beneath it red with blood.

They were gruesome pictures, but she had seen many similar ones. Hunting was a required rite of manhood around here. Practically everyone hunted, even some of the woman. It was the most common subject for discussion, more popular than farming, tractors and crops put together. The local schools were even let out the day that hunting season officially opened.

She put everything back in the box. Kane could worry about retrieving his past when and if he decided to. She wasn't going to worry about the box. Or the coat.

There were two men seated on the moss-covered log. A rifle was propped up against the log between them. The grass rustled from the dog sniffing around the fence row behind them.

"You ever going to get around to fixing that old barn of yours?" one of the men asked.

The other man scratched a grizzled cheek that protruded from a wad of chewing tobacco. He spat a brown stream of tobacco into the weeds between his feet and took his time before answering. "Nope," he said. "Not this year. No sense getting' in a hurry. There's always next year."

He tilted a small, dented flask of whiskey up to his lips. He drank deeply and set the bottle down between his knees again before he reached up to adjust the battered, sweat-stained brim of the hat he was wearing.

"I expect I did pretty good this past year, all in all," he went on. "Haven't been sick a day. Wife puts meals on the table when I'm hungry. She lets me hunt when I want to. A man can't ask for much more'n that, I reckon. Yep, nothing better than being out in the woods." His eyes, one brown and one blue, squinted at the clear blue sky above him.

The man beside him had nothing to say as he looked down at the grass and nodded his head in silent agreement. The dog suddenly let out a deep woof and scratched at something in the weeds.

"Why, you old coon dog, what're you diggin' at now?" Cyril Clayton, Blue to those who knew him, called out. "Hey, Ol' Red," he yelled sharply at the dog in his gravelly voice. "Get your sorry carcass over here."

Both men watched the dog for a few moments.

"Never know what you're going to find in these woods," was Blue's next observation. "Probably a damned mouse or a mole. That's the worst dog I ever saw for digging."

The dog, apparently having lost interest in whatever it was, finally came bounding back. Blue continued to squint at the weeds where the dog had been scratching. He took another long drink of whiskey, lowered the bottle and shifted his eyes to the right for a brief moment.

"Like that girl," Blue said.

Both men were now staring off at the distant line of trees that bordered the field in front of them. "Terrible thing that was. I can still see her yeller hair shinin' under the dirt and the leaves. She was white as a sheet. And the blood- "

Blue's words trailed off as he shook his head. "There's something I've been meanin' to give you." He spat again with expert precision, then twisted his body as he began to dig deeply into the pocket of worn brown canvas work pants. "I found this when I found the girl."

Neither man looked at each other, but the shiny metal glinted briefly as the object exchanged hands. "It was a ways off from the body," Blue said quietly. "I recognized it right off. I don't expect there are too many around like that one."

The other man slipped the knife into his shirt pocket. He bowed his head and continued to stare at the ground between his feet, his face hardening along with his thoughts.

He turned his face to the side, away from Blue. "So you never told anyone you found it?"

"Nope," was Blue's succinct reply. "We've hunted together, drank together and you've covered my back more'n once when I needed it."

"Yeah, we've hunted a lot over the years."

"I didn't say nothin' about it. And I don't intend to. I'll take it to my grave."

"I believe that, Blue," the other man said. "And I'm obliged."

"Don't mean nothin' atall. I'm just seein' that it gets back to its rightful owner, is all." Blue's words were a little slurred now. Cyril Clayton liked his whiskey. "You know me. I'm good at keeping quiet about things." The hint of pride in his voice reached even his mismatched eyes.

"Well, I'm glad for the favor, Blue. I really am. But I can't take the chance that you'll always keep quiet about it."

There was surprise in Cyril Clayton's eyes as he turned his head. A split second later comprehension dawned.

There was no anger in it. No malice. Cyril Clayton had been his friend for more years than he could count. He did Blue a favor and made it quick. A split second did not give Blue enough time to react. Or to plead. A split second that was all the life left to him before the rock bashed in his skull.

Luck was with him in the convenience of a nearby abandoned well. A well deep enough to hide a body forever.

He almost smiled there in the cool shade of the trees. An easier, handier grave there never was. And Blue would be in the woods where he was happiest. No better place for Blue to be than out here in the woods forever.

Chapter 7

The scents of freshly-mown grass and lilac blossoms just opening drifted through the open windows. Spring was in full bloom and the weather was about as perfect as it could be.

Jesse, along with Josh and Abby, had worked hard all morning. The least Jenna could do was to feed them, she thought as she set a pitcher of iced tea on the table. Next to it she set a pitcher of freshly-squeezed lemonade. A platter of sliced ham, roast beef and fresh bakery bread were next, followed by the cole slaw and potato salad she had put together last night.

She sliced a tomato, thinking about the garden she would put in, which meant freshly-picked tomatoes and lettuce. Along with carrots, onions and potatoes that hadn't been sprayed with chemicals. An herb garden would be nice, too.

Officially, she could consider this the first meal in her new home. It was a comfortable old house, small but just big enough for her. A porch covered half the front of the house and wrapped around one side. The yard was shaded by big trees and there were neighbors within view, which was much different from the other house where she had been completely isolated.

They had gotten an early start and made two trips in a rented moving truck. The truck was now sitting empty in the driveway while Jenna put the finishing touches on lunch. She had spent the most pleasant day she could remember in a long time. She enjoyed spending time with Jesse, Josh and Abby.

"Lunch looks good," Jesse said as he walked into the kitchen. "Is anyone else as starved as I am?" he asked.

Josh had followed him in. "I am, Uncle Jesse." Abby was right behind Josh.

"It was really nice of all of you to help me today," Jenna said after they had all taken a seat at the table.

"It was nice of you to make us lunch," Jesse said.

Jenna glanced at Jesse sitting across the table and experienced a strange sense of satisfaction as he filled his plate then passed the food around the table to her. Kane would have turned up his nose at her lunch even before tasting it. He had let her know early in the marriage that he didn't consider sandwiches to be much of a meal.

But Jesse enjoyed her food and more than that, he let her know how much he appreciated the effort that she had put into making it. It was the same with Josh and Abby. Obviously, they were used to enjoying meals together. The relaxed conversation flowed easily.

The three of them had shown up at her door early that morning. Jesse was dressed more casually than he dressed for the office. He was wearing jeans and a comfortable-looking faded plaid shirt. His shirt sleeves were rolled back and his shirt was open in the front to reveal a gray T-shirt beneath it. His shoulders were broad under the faded shirt, the muscles of his chest defined beneath the T-shirt. She had caught herself staring at him more than once during the day. Like now.

She couldn't help stealing glances at Jesse every now and then. He had made a distractingly appealing picture for her from the moment she had opened her door to see him standing on her front porch with the early morning sunlight filtering down on him as he waited for her.

He was a hard worker. Josh was a hard worker, too. Jesse had gotten her mower going, and had even brought a can of gas with him. Josh had spent part of the morning cutting the grass for her, which had grown thick and green after the recent rains.

Josh clearly idolized his uncle. It was easy to see that the attention he received from Jesse was important to him and would help him grown into a decent, well-adjusted young man with the right kind of values and priorities.

And Abby was, well, Abby. Unique and very complex beneath her quiet exterior, Abby saw things differently. She saw things that other people took for granted or never saw at all. Jenna had come to understand autism in a different way. For one thing, there were widely varying degrees of autism. For another, the condition was not completely understood, even by the experts.

Abby definitely had a different way of perceiving things sometimes. Right now, Abby was reaching for another piece of bakery bread.

"You like the bread, Abby?" Jenna asked.

Abby nodded.

"Would you like me to teach you to make homemade bread?" Jenna asked. "My grandmother taught me. You see that big bowl up on the shelf? I used to watch my grandmother make bread in that bowl when I was a little girl. I could teach you if you like."

Jenna had quickly gotten used to Abby's ways, Jesse thought as he lifted his glass of iced tea. He could see that Abby liked the idea of spending time with Jenna. Abby liked Jenna. And Jenna was good with Abby. She seemed to understand her and to accept her just the way she was.

Jesse listened as Jenna talked about how many tulips there had been in her grandmother's yard when she was little and then described for Abby why a certain flower was called touch-me-nots.

"If you touch the seed pods when they're ripe, even a little, they'll spring open and the seeds will scatter everywhere."

Jesse's gaze strayed over the mass of gold curls caught up loosely on top of Jenna's head, down to the stray tendrils drifting softly about her face and neck. He found himself wanting to free her hair of the confining hairclip and letting those curls tumble down past her shoulders. He had seen her hair undone before and it reached nearly to her waist. She had beautiful hair. It had always fascinated him.

She was talking about the bakery in town, planning a trip down there sometime with both the kids. He was more than a little surprised when Abby started asking questions about the bakery and when they could go.

Leaning back in his chair, Jesse continued to watch Jenna. He took another sip of tea and couldn't help smiling, too, as she laughed at something Abby and Josh were telling her.

His gaze lowered to her mouth. He had to be careful now because more than once today he had experienced an urge to kiss her. And that wasn't good. Not good at all. Remember the flowers, he reminded himself. Touch-me-nots.

He didn't lie to himself. He was fighting an attraction to her. He would continue to fight it. He knew that Jenna didn't want the complication of a romantic involvement and the last thing he wanted to do was to ruin their friendship. A friendship that seemed to have deepened in some inexplicable way these past few weeks.

55

But that didn't change the fact that he had found himself drawn to her all day. And the more time he spent with her, he realized, the stronger the pull. She was dressed casually today, for hard work. Not like she dressed for the office. He had found the effect more than a little distracting.

There were no high heels today, but sturdy hiking boots. Though why he should find the boots sexy as hell was beyond him. The faded, well-worn jeans she was wearing hugged every curve. That didn't help, either. Neither did the soft blue top she had on. It drew attention to the soft swell of her breasts and emphasized, rather than concealed, the contrast of narrow waist and flat belly. Equally distracting was the way the top perfectly matched the color of her eyes.

She had nearly taken his breath away when she had answered the door that morning. Her hair had been hanging loose below her shoulders before she went back in the house to gather it up. Those gold-tinged curls had been a little wild and unruly as if she had just gotten out of bed.

Bed. Another dangerous area. He pushed that thought aside because it took him down a road he shouldn't be traveling on at all. His imagination could conjure all kinds of things if he thought about Jenna in bed. Like the warm, soft feel of her skin and the scent of her that was like a field of wild flowers, a scent that seemed to have some kind of intoxicating power over him lately.

They had accidentally brushed hands earlier that morning. He had taken a heavy box from her and what should have been a casual touch had sent a charge of electricity running through him that had just about brought him to his knees. He wasn't going to let that happen again.

Jenna glanced over to see a thoughtful, frowning Jesse staring at her from across the table. As if it had a life of its own, a flame ignited low in her stomach. It was a completely involuntary reaction and something entirely against her will. She might not be able to completely ignore it, but she was determined to at least get it under control.

It was like that moment earlier when they had accidentally touched hands. She had not been prepared for the touch or her reaction to it. The sensation had traveled up her arm at light speed, sending shock waves to her very core.

She was at a loss to understand it. She had never felt anything like that. Not with any man.

She had been inexperienced when she had married Kane. More than once, he had accused her of being frigid. And the truth was that there were times when she had wondered if maybe she didn't have a problem with intimacy. Kane had been selfish and demanding when it came to sex or any other kind of closeness in their marriage. At times, he had even seemed punishing. After a while, she had grown to dread that part of their relationship. So why was she reacting this way with Jesse? She was still wondering as she glanced at Jesse again.

"You have a fenced yard now," Jesse was saying to her. "Have you considered getting yourself a dog?"

"Actually I have thought about it," Jenna replied.

It would be nice to have someone greet her when she came home from work each day. She was not so isolated now, but she was still living alone. Which was why she had signed up for the women's self-defense classes that Jesse was going to start teaching next week.

"There are a couple of dogs in the pound," Jesse told her. "Maybe we could go look at them one day next week."

"All right," she said. Abby certainly looked as if she like the idea. "But I could probably use some help picking one out."

"I'll bet Josh and Abby would like to help you pick out a dog," Jesse said with a smile.

Jesse would feel a lot better if Jenna did get herself a dog. With a killer running loose, he was concerned about her living out here all alone. He would feel even better when he got the new locks put on her doors.

"After we eat, we'll put your boxes and furniture in the rooms where you want them," he said as he set his napkin on the table.

"You've all done enough already," Jenna started to protest. "Really. More than enough. I can take care of the rest."

"You're going to carry that dresser upstairs all by yourself? And your bed and mattresses?"

It did seem silly for her to think about accomplishing those things by herself when they were willing to help.

"All right," she relented with a sigh. "I have to admit, it would be hard getting those things moved by myself."

Jesse was the kind of man who kept at a job until it was finished. He had already made up his mind that he was going to finish helping her move. She had to get used to the idea that he wasn't helping her because he expected something in return. Jesse was helping her merely for the sake of helping and he was, she could see, instilling those values in Josh and Abby. They worked well together. They helped each other out, respected each other and genuinely enjoyed each other's company. It was the way she had always imagined a family should be.

She was also becoming aware of something else. She was aware that she had been looking at Jesse differently today. She had already decided that he was a man of integrity and inner strength. She admired those things. But it was more. She was beginning to notice small things as well. Like how his dark hair curled in a slightly unruly fashion over his shirt collar, making her want to touch the ebony strands that looked so silky soft in the sunlight. Or the strength in the hand resting on the table before him. Or how, when he smiled, it was like the sun coming out of the clouds.

She frowned and shook herself mentally. Such observations weren't doing her any good. She had never been the kind of woman who was attracted to a man simply on the basis of good looks. And Jesse was definitely that. Good-looking.

But the truth was that her attraction to Jesse went beyond just the physical. It was his thoughtfulness, his easy laugh and the way that laugh reached his eyes. Even his patient way with Josh and Abby was something that she found very appealing.

In the office, Jesse was attractive enough. But his casual Jesse with the faded shirt and the jeans clinging to long, strongly-muscled legs invoked a response in her that she simply didn't know how to deal with.

As she got up from the table, she told herself that admitting her attraction was the first step in dealing with it. She would control it, of course. She was not the kind of woman who let those things control her.

She was finding, however, that control was easier said than done. After the food and the dishes had been put away and Josh and Abby went outside, she found herself alone in the kitchen with Jesse. She was folding a dish towel when she heard him say behind her, "You need a light bulb in that outlet."

She turned to look up at the empty light fixture in the ceiling.

"Do you have light bulbs?" he asked and looked around at the boxes stacked in the kitchen. "If you do, you probably don't know where they would be."

"I do," she answered. "They're right here in this box." She leaned over and opened a box marked kitchen and found the bulbs inside.

When she straightened, she caught Jesse watching her with a look that caused another fluttery sensation deep inside her.

58

"I'll go get the step ladder. I left it on the porch, he said and abruptly left the room.

He returned with the ladder and replaced the bulb.

"Let's check the rest of them," he said, climbing down from the ladder. "You don't want to be taking care of this chore after it's dark."

There was an outlet in the bathroom and another one in her bedroom closet that needed a new bulb. In the close confines of the closet Jenna avoided looking directly at Jesse. She was absolutely not going to get close enough to accidentally touch him again. It wasn't that she didn't trust him. She wasn't sure she could trust herself any more. Not where Jesse was concerned.

She remained silent as he stood on the ladder. She was very much aware of his scent. It wasn't perfumy like some men. He smelled like clean laundry and fresh air and there was something else beneath it that was very male. And very, very appealing.

They were standing close together and his nearness was making her feel a strange, breathless sensation. Even though they weren't touching, every nerve ending in her body seemed to have come alive with a kind of glowing awareness.

The husky quality of his voice drew her even deeper into awareness as he talked casually about putting in a garden and about changing the locks. He would come back later, he said, with new locks and put them on for her.

And that's when Jenna made a mistake. She dared to look up at him. She watched him reach over his head. She stared at his frowning concentration. Her gaze lowered to his mouth. Against her will, she found herself wondering what his kisses would be like. And that made her wonder what kind of a lover Jesse would be. She imagined the passion simmering beneath the surface brought to life, an artist's passion, and suspected that gentleness from Jesse would be just as devastating as the unleashed passion would be.

She looked away as he got down from the ladder. To steady himself, he braced a hand on the wall behind her. He wasn't talking at the moment, but she felt his gaze on her.

Helplessly, she looked up at him. He still didn't speak. His gaze remained on her, changed in some unfathomable way.

She knew immediately that she had made a mistake in looking up at him. She had not meant anything with that look, but awareness flared like a brush fire between them. Even in the dim light of the closet she was aware of something new in his eyes. She sensed a struggle in him.

59

He suddenly frowned and shifted his gaze, studying the wall behind her. He shook the closet door at her back.

"I've noticed the closet door sticks," he said, his voice lower and huskier than usual.

"I've noticed that, too."

"This one, I think," he breathed, still frowning at the door.

She couldn't speak. She could only nod her head. They were standing so close that she could feel the heat from his body. Right through her clothes. His scent wrapped itself around her. Masculine. Seductive.

"I'll take care of that, too, when I come back."

What else did she want him to take care of when he returned? She couldn't help the thought from forming. But she remained silent as his gaze returned to her face.

"Do you have more light bulbs, Jenna? We ought to- " he began. His voice was very soft, very hushed. It trailed away before he finished.

He closed his eyes and his frown deepened. She saw the muscles in his jaw grow tense. She held out the box of light bulbs, forgetting the danger of his hand touching hers. But that's just what happened.

It was a light touch, flesh barely grazing flesh, a mere brushing of fingers. But it had the searing power of a bolt of lightning, an unexpected bolt. She couldn't have uttered a word if her life depended on it. Jesse wasn't saying anything, either. Almost imperceptibly he leaned closer. She held her breath.

And then, suddenly, they were jolted out of the moment by the sound of Josh and Abby arguing in the hallway outside her bedroom. They quickly moved away from each other, just as if they were guilty of being caught doing something they shouldn't be doing.

"Abby, there aren't any such things," she heard Josh say.

Jenna followed Jesse out of the closet. She was still fighting to regain her composure. The last thing she wanted was for Jesse to realize how deeply he had just affected her. How much he was still affecting her. Josh and Abby were still arguing when Jesse set the step ladder down.

"Uncle Jesse, tell Abby there are no such things as ghosts."

"Ghosts?" Jesse queried, raising a dark brow as he looked at Abby.

Jesse was being very careful not to look at Jenna. She was still very much in his thoughts, however. His reaction to her in the closet had been like a wild fire that had gotten out of control way too fast. He had managed to get the outward flames under control, but the fire was still smoldering deep down where no one could see it.

"Abby said there were ghosts in the other house," Josh went on. "She says she felt them there. She says there aren't any ghosts here."

That surprised Jenna a little. Kane had said he was aware of ghosts there, too. Was it just a child's imagination? Or did Abby have some deeper sense of awareness?

As for awareness, she was still very much aware of Jesse standing beside her. She had avoided looking at him, but now she chanced a quick glance at him from beneath her lashes.

"H'm," Jesse muttered as he folded the ladder. "As long as there's none here, that's a good thing. Right, Ab?" he said, half teasingly while Abby solemnly nodded.

Before they left the bedroom, Jesse's gaze met Jenna's once, briefly, conveying nothing that she could identify. Nothing at all.

"I'll check the other light fixtures," he said before he left the room, taking the step ladder with him.

Retreating to the kitchen, Jenna set a plate of cookies on the table. Abby and Josh were both reaching for a cookie when Jesse returned. She heard his cell phone ring and watched him pull the phone out of his pocket.

"Yeah."

He listened to someone on the other end of the phone and then asked, "Missing how long?"

Jenna waited until Jesse had put the phone away. Hoping there was not another murder victim, she asked. "What happened?"

"Cyril Clayton's wife just reported him as missing. He went hunting yesterday and never returned. Dell wants me to come in and fill out a report."

"Josh and Abby can stay here with me," Jenna offered "Maybe the three of us could run out to the pound and look at any dogs they might have there."

"All right," Jesse said. "They would like that. When I get back, we can finish up here."

The pound was just a couple of cages set up in the back of Buck Hendley's machine shed. He also ran a car repair shop in there. There were two dogs. One was a small fluffy white dog whose entire body wagged back and forth at the first sight of Josh and Abby. The other dog was a larger lab mix, just skin and bones with sticks and burrs matted in his fur. But he looked at Jenna with big brown needy eyes that melted her heart. It was too hard to decide which dog to take, so, to the delight of Josh and Abby, she took them both.

They had to run across town to get cages. After loading up the dogs, they dropped them off at the vet's office for checkups, grooming and shots. The little white dog was a female, so Jenna also arranged to have the dog neutered. They were leaving the vet's office when Jesse called and said he would be later than he had anticipated, but that he would pick up pizza and bring it back for dinner.

Several hours later, Jesse realized he had spent more time in town than he had intended. After filling out the missing person report, he went uptown to do some checking. By the time he finished talking to several people around town who knew Cyril Clayton, the hardware store was closed. He still hadn't gotten those new locks for Jenna's doors. He should have made that a priority.

It was almost dark when he pulled into the parking lot of Pizza Plus to pick up dinner. He still had no answers. No one knew what had happened to Cyril Clayton. Or his dog.

Chapter 8

The sun was going down, but if she hurried, she would be on her way before dark. Jenna walked through the empty rooms of the house for the last time. The wooden floors gave back the hollow echo of her footsteps. Other than that, the house was silent. Eerily so. She couldn't help but think about Abby saying that there were ghosts here.

She paused in the bedroom doorway. The sun was slanting in through the only window in the room. The window glass was old and full of distortions and imperfections. Just like the mirror on the old chest of drawers. It was the only piece of furniture left in the room. It had been passed down several generations in Kane's family. A treasured heirloom although Kane had not yet come to get it.

Jenna had always hated the chest of drawers. The dark wood was covered with scratches and the mirror in the door was spotted and cloudy. The door itself did not close properly, but would work its way open in spite of every effort to keep it closed.

She crossed the room and stood before the chest of drawers. When she had been packing, she had dropped her jewelry box and the entire contents had scattered across the floor. One of her earrings was missing. It was from a pair that her mother had given her. She hoped that it had fallen behind the chest of drawers. She would get the earring if it was there, and then she would leave, closing and locking the door behind her for the last time.

With some effort she pulled the heavy piece of furniture away from the wall. The earring was nowhere in sight. She sighed, disappointed. She would have to keep looking for the earring at home.

She left the chest of drawers where it was. No sense in expending all that effort to push it back against the wall since Kane would be coming for it sooner or later. One of the legs was loose anyway, so moving it around anymore than necessary wasn't doing it any good.

She turned and stared towards the door then stopped short. She had seen, as she turned, a narrow beam of sunlight slanting across the room.

She frowned as she walked over to the door that connected the bedroom with the bathroom and discovered that the light was coming through a small hole in the door. Dust motes drifted slowly in the bright, pencil-thin ray of light.

She pulled the door open and looked at it from the other side. The hold had been precisely drilled in one corner of the wooden door panels. There was a faint dusting of sawdust on the ledge below it.

As she realized that the hole had been carefully and deliberately drilled, there also came another disturbing thought. Had someone been secretly watching her? If that was true, who would it have been? Kane had been the only other person living here, but he had moved out some time ago.

She tried to recall when the dresser had been put there. She had told Kane to take the dresser but he had never come for it. Was it because he knew it was covering the evidence of the hole? But that wasn't likely. Kane could have easily patched up the hold before she was even aware of its existence.

She thought back over the time she had lived here with Kane. More often than not, when she had demanded some privacy, some boundaries, he had ridden right over those boundaries. Was Kane also capable of this violation? And if not Kane, then who? Had someone else been in the house? Had the hole been drilled before or after Kane had moved out?

She spun around, startled when she realized she wasn't alone. She hadn't heard a car. She hadn't even heard footsteps, but Kane was standing in the doorway watching her.

"Why didn't you say something? Why didn't you let me know you were standing there?"

Kane remained silent as he filled the bedroom doorway.

"I hate it when you sneak up on me like that."

"I didn't sneak up on you," he said. "I was down at the pond when you drove up."

"What were you doing down there?"

"Fishing. What else? What are you doing here?" he asked.

There was a pond a little distance behind the house. A dirt road led to it and you couldn't see a car parked down there from the house.

Kane did fish down there a lot, but Jenna was still thinking about the hole. She didn't know which was worse. Believing that Kane had made the hole or that someone else might have been in the house watching her. Of the two possibilities, she decided that it was more likely that Kane was guilty.

"What is that?" Her hand gestured toward the ray of light.

"What is *what?*" he asked.

"That hole in the door. That someone has deliberately drilled."

His eyes followed the tell-tale beam of light and then shifted back to her. He frowned as if he didn't understand what she was talking about. And then his brows lifted as he asked, "You think I did that?"

"Who else *could* have done it?"

"It's been a long time since you kicked me out, you know. How do I know how it got there or who else has been in here?"

She did not fail to note the implication in his words.

She continued to watch his reaction. He was watching her just as carefully.

"It's an old house," he said dismissively. "Maybe it was bugs. Maybe the wood is cracked. How should I know?"

"It is not a crack and it wasn't bugs. Someone drilled the hole. There is sawdust on the ledge below it."

As if he hadn't heard a word she said, he tried explaining it away again. "It's probably been there for years."

She shook her head. "No. This dresser hasn't always been against that wall. I would have noticed the light coming through it before."

A normal reaction on Kane's part, Jenna thought, would have been curiosity. At least. Which should have made him check the hold himself. And concern for her safety, if he ever truly felt that emotion, would have made him wonder who had made it.

But Kane didn't look at the door again. In fact, he didn't seem to be concerned about it in the least.

"Who do you think could have made that hole?" she asked him. "Who else would have access to this house?" But she already knew the answer. The entire Blackwell family would have access to the house. And that included Kane and Randal Blackwell.

Kane's brother, Randal, had threatened Jenna during the divorce. According to Kane himself, Randal wanted to do something to her to teach her a lesson. That's what loyalty meant to the Blackwells. As twisted as it was, Kane still couldn't find fault in his brother's behavior. He never did. He seemed to treat the whole issue as a huge joke.

"I don't know how it got there," Kane went on. "But it wasn't my doing. Why would I do it?"

"I don't know," she shot back. "Maybe you got some kind of sick thrill over secretly watching me when I didn't know you were there." She was getting really upset now as the seriousness of the situation sank in. Especially in light of the fact that there was a killer out there somewhere.

"You're wrong," he said, eyeing her coldly now. "Because I never did it. I never even knew that the hole was there."

Of course she had no way of knowing for certain f he was telling her the truth or not. Kane had lied to her in the past. She thought he was lying now.

"The hole was carefully drilled," she repeated. "And the sawdust isn't that old."

His expression turned sarcastic. "Oh, so you're an expert in forensics now." He sneered and said, "Your boyfriend been teaching you?"

"My boyfriend? What are you talking about?"

As Kane continued to look at her, his mouth straightened into an unpleasant line. "You know very well. The one who helped you move." His tone turned accusing. "You were seen."

"Seen doing what? Moving? I hope you don't expect me to defend myself because someone helped me move."

"Well, now I know why you refused *my* help."

"For your information, Jesse happens to be my friend."

For a moment something dark glittered in Kane's eyes. "Really," he said flatly. "And being friends includes overnight visits?"

Kane's jealousy had been one of the biggest issues in their marriage. Right now, however, Jenna was wondering how they had gotten so quickly off the subject and why they were discussing Jesse at all.

"We were talking about that hole in the door. I just want the truth, Kane."

"It's a damned hole. Why the hell do you need to overreact over everything?"

"You think it's overreacting when I find out that someone may be watching me?" She threw her hands in the air. "Why should that surprise me? You thought I was overreacting when I was threatened by your brother, too."

"Are you trying to say that Rand made that hole now?"

It was amazing how fast Kane could leap to conclusions and put words in her mouth.

"Well, in that case," he said with an ugly smirk. "Why don't you get your detective *friend* over here to dust for fingerprints? And maybe he can run a DNA test while he's at it."

She was angry now. Over his nasty attitude which she believed was covering his guilt. She shook her head. "I can't believe you would do something like this."

"What? You're accusing *me*? Of what? Of being some kind of pervert?"

"You moved that dresser the day you moved out. You put it right there." She was remembering that day now. She had wondered at the time why Kane was arranging furniture. He had never been interested in decorating before that.

"Well, you can believe what you want to believe," he said.

"No," she said. "I don't want to believe that you could do something like this. But I do know- "

"You know," he interrupted her harshly. "Everything there is to know. As usual."

"Obviously I don't. I don't know when someone is spying on me."

"You don't have any proof that that's what happened."

"Yes, Kane. I do." She flung her hand out toward the beam of light again. "There is the proof."

It was pointless to continue to argue with him. She knew very well that she was fighting a losing battle. Kane was never going to admit the truth. Being caught in a lie had never shaken the truth from Kane in all the time she had known him. Not even when he had been caught cheating on her.

With her teeth clamped tightly together, Jenna spun around and left the bedroom. She grabbed her purse and her car keys off the kitchen counter and left the house. The sun had already disappeared into the trees to the west.

Chapter 9

Jenna blinked several times, then closed her eyes for a few moments. She arched her back and stretched. Her muscles had begun to ache a long time ago. She had ignored the discomfort earlier, but her muscles were beginning to stiffen painfully. Besides, it was getting harder to focus and the words were beginning to blur before her. It would be easy to miss something if she kept going.

She settled back in the hard wooden library chair, flexed her shoulders and lifted one hand to massage the back of her neck. She didn't know how late it was. She couldn't see the clock from where she was sitting, but it felt late. Beyond the tall library windows, the sunlight had mellowed to a dee gold.

She had been leaning over the microfilm machine since before lunchtime. Besides the librarian, Jenna was the only person in the library. Until she heard the little bells jangle as someone opened the door.

"Hey." Jesse pulled up a chair and sat down beside her. "Do you know it's almost 5:00?"

"Is it?" she asked, surprised.

"It is," he said quietly. "You've been at it for more than five hours. Not to mention the time you spent at the courthouse this morning."

I didn't realize it was so late," she said as she removed the roll of microfilm from the machine and carefully rewound it. No wonder her back ached and she was having trouble focusing. "What's it like outside?" she asked.

"It's getting pretty cold. The bank said 53 degrees."

"I thought it was supposed to stay warm. Good thing I thought to put a jacket in my car." She placed the microfilm in the empty space in its box then put the box back into the drawer. "I got a little sidetracked," she confessed.

"So what got you sidetracked?"

"I had been researching local crimes for you and I came across the newspaper reports of the murder of my ex-husband's brother." She frowned thoughtfully. "Then I spent some time studying the transcripts of the trial at the courthouse. There were some discrepancies in the records, it seems."

"That's not unusual," he said. "Things can be pretty confusing after a murder. People are upset. Emotionally distraught. Maybe not thinking clearly. And newspaper reports can be notoriously inaccurate."

"Yes," she agreed. "But there are a few things that don't make sense to me."

Jesse waited for her to go on.

"I was under the impression that the actual murder was committed in an upstairs bedroom. The court records say that the murder itself was committed in the basement but that the body was found in the closet of an upstairs bedroom. Why would anyone do that? Why kill someone and then hide the body two flights of stairs up from where the murder actually occurred? You would think that the basement would be a better hiding place."

"I don't know," Jesse replied thoughtfully. "But you're right. On the surface it doesn't make much sense. Maybe the victim was shot in the basement but was still alive. He could have made his way upstairs or been forced up there with threats. Nothing was brought up in court about it?"

She shook her head. "No. I have considered everything you just said. But there were five bullet wounds. Wouldn't there have been a blood trail from the basement to the bedroom?"

"You would think so," Jesse said, agreeing with her.

"Well, it gets even more confusing," she went on. "One newspaper account said that Kane, along with his father and his brother Randal, discovered the body. Another report stated that it was only Kane and his father. But- " And here she looked even more confused. "The court reports have a statement from Randal Blackwell saying that he had been in the house looking for his brother just days before the discovery of the body, that he had been there twice actually.

In the house. And, not finding his brother, he left, not knowing that he was already dead upstairs.

"That is hard to believe," Jenna continued. "Because no one in that family can make a move without the others knowing about it. They keep pretty close tabs on each other. We are talking about a period of almost three weeks between the time of the murder and when the body was actually found. I find that amazing in itself. In any case, if Randal Blackwell was in the house, why didn't he see any blood? Or realize that something was wrong? It's hard to think that almost three weeks could have passed before they realized that he was even missing.

"I wasn't there and I don't know all the facts," she went on. "In fact, I don't know any of the facts. It was a long time ago and no one talks about the murder. Of course, it has to be a terribly painful memory for all of them, but I am getting a real sense that there is something more buried back there."

"You're right, Jenna. It doesn't make a lot of sense. And it does raise a lot of questions. A murder can dredge up all kinds of things. From what you have told me about the family, there's a good chance that there are some rotten bones nobody wants to have dug up. After thirteen years, it's hard to say what might have happened. Even if you could get anyone to talk, we're talking about a murder that happened a long time ago. People's memories tend to fade and get distorted. What was the motive?" Jesse asked.

"Some antique coins had been stolen from the victim, so officially robbery was the motive. But I haven't seen anything that says the coins were ever recovered."

Jesse thought over what she had told him. "If the coins weren't found, then that could have been disputed in court," he told her.

"There's more," Jenna went on. "As I said, the body wasn't discovered for almost three weeks. That's a long time."

Jesse raised his brows now.

"Do you see what I'm getting at?" she asked him.

He nodded slowly. "The evidence of decomposition after that amount of time would have been hard not to notice, to say the least. For anyone near that house. Unless the weather stayed below freezing."

"I've already thought of that," she said. "I checked the weather reports. There was a warm spell, warmer than usual. It was sustained over a two-week period. I'm familiar with the February thaw in this area because that's what causes the sap to rise in the maple trees so that it can be collected for maple syrup. The Blackwells always make maple syrup in February," she went on thoughtfully. "It seems to me that they would have been in close contact at that time."

Jesse was impressed. She would make one hell of a detective.

"Not only that," she went on. "But if the house was cold without a wood fire being kept up- I mean, I don't know for sure, but most old houses around here use wood stoves for heat. Someone would have noticed."

"There's one more thing," she said. "There was a dramatic scene in the courtroom at the end of the trial where the cousin who was accused of the murder vowed vengeance on all the Blackwells when he got out of prison."

"Vengeance for what?"

"I don't know," Jenna replied. "It's just one more question that meets with evasive answers."

She began collecting her papers. "Well, now that I'm curious- " She hesitated a moment before she added, "I thought I would go up there on my way home."

"Go up where?" Jesse asked, his eyes narrowing slightly. He hoped she wasn't going to say what he thought she was going to say.

"The house where the murder occurred. Nobody lives there anymore."

"Isn't that technically called trespassing?"

"Technically, maybe," Jenna conceded. "But I have never been up there and I have always wanted to see the house for myself."

Jesse was frowning now.

She shrugged, dismissing his obvious concern. People rummage through these old houses around here all the time. Nobody thinks twice about it. I probably won't even be able to get into the house. More than likely it's locked up."

"You were thinking about going inside?"

"I was," she confessed. "Yes, if it's open."

She saw the look on his face. "It's the perfect time," she explained. "Kane and his brother are away on a fishing trip. They won't be back for a few days. I'll just have a quick look around, pick up something for dinner and go home."

He would have talked her out of it if he thought that it would do any good, but he suspected his efforts would be a waste of time. He wasn't about to let her go up there alone, however.

"You mean *we'll* just have a quick look around, and then we'll pick up something for dinner and go home." There was no way he was going to let her go prowling around by herself in the middle of nowhere, this close to dark with a killer possibly stalking future victims.

"Jesse, you don't have to do that. It isn't a big deal. Really."

The way he sat back in his chair and crossed his arms over his chest made her realize that he wasn't going to back down no matter what she said.

"I owe you a dinner anyway," he reminded her.

"You already paid me back. You helped me move. And don't forget about the pizza."

"That's true," he said. "But you fixed lunch for us. So I still owe you a meal. And we need to be going soon." He checked his watch. "It's going to be dark in two hours."

He got up from his chair, giving her no chance to refuse his offer.

"What about a baby sitter?"

"School let out early. Gussie Hester is already at the house making dinner for the kids. And I have my cell phone." He tapped his pocket.

"All right," she relented. "We'll go together."

"We can check out the house," he said over his shoulder. "After that you go home while I make a quick run down to Collver and pick up Chinese. How does that sound?"

"Chinese food?"

Oh, yeah. The Chinese food did it. H could tell he had found a weak spot.

"I haven't had Chinese food in forever," she said as she stood up and slung the strap of her purse over her shoulder. "But first I want to make a quick stop at the bakery so you can take some brownies home for Josh and Abby from me."

She gathered up the last of her notes. The dates of the murders were written on one of the pieces of paper. "I checked out everything you suggested. And some other things I thought of. There were no weather patterns or similarities that I could find. And nothing happened on those days that stands out. But I'll keep looking."

"There's a pattern somewhere," Jesse said as he opened the library door for her. "We just have to keep looking until we find it."

Stubborn. Tenacious. Intuitive. Jenna would make a damned good detective, was Jesse's thought as they stood in line at the bakery behind a woman who was waiting for her order.

The woman stood at the high counter with her back to them. As if suddenly sensing their presence, the woman spun around and stared hard at Jenna for several long moments.

She was a plain-looking woman whose harsh features could have used some softening with a little makeup, he thought. Her coat was a drab brown. Her gray-streaked hair was almost the same color as the coat. There was nothing, not even a smile, to brighten or relieve the woman's washed-out features. Except in the eyes, Jesse decided. They bordered on being predatory.

In the first unguarded moments after she had turned, Jesse detected unveiled hostility in the woman's expression as she recognized Jenna. The look was quickly replaced by a smile as insincere as any he had ever seen.

"Hello, Jenna," the woman greeted, the smile pasted on now like a mask that she was used to hiding behind. Those pale eyes shifted from Jenna to Jesse as if they belonged to a hungry cat in search of prey and searching for a weakness.

Trapped into the obligatory introduction, Jenna said, "Vidia, this is Jesse Logan. Jesse, this is Vidia Blackwell."

"I'm happy to meet you, Mr. Logan. So how is small town life after Chicago?" Vidia wanted to know.

"It's a definite change," was Jesse's reply.

Vidia laughed as if she had just discovered a secret that she intended keeping to herself. It came as no surprise to Jenna that Vidia knew that Jesse was from Chicago. The woman made it her business to know everything there was to know in Alder Grove.

Her probing eyes shifted back to Jenna. "Working late?" she asked.

Jenna nodded. "Yes, actually we were." She realized very well that Vidia was fishing for gossip. She also knew what that gossip would be about.

"I heard you had moved, Jenna. How do you like your new place?"

Jenna managed to suppressed the urge to mimic Vidia's over-sweet tone with a sarcastic, "Love it, Vidia." But she said politely instead, "It's very nice."

Irita Langston, who ran the bakery, came out of the back room and stepped up to the counter. "Here's your receipt, Vidia. I'll have your birthday cake ready at noon on Friday. You be sure and tell Rand happy birthday for me."

"Why don't you tell him that yourself? The fish fry stars at 4:00."

"Well, maybe I'll do that," Irita said.

Vidia soon left the bakery and Jenna stepped up to the counter to place her order.

"I'll have a dozen brownies. And throw in two of those decorated cookies, too, if you would." She pointed to the ones she meant.

Irita put the brownies and the cookies into two white paper bags and smoothed her apron a little self-consciously while Jenna counted out change. The woman was still watching them when they stepped out into the deepening spring dusk.

They drove slowly along the winding gravel road that had a surface as rough as an old scrub board. The gravel had washed badly in several places due to the recent rains. A mile and a half from the main road, they crossed a one-lane bridge. The road continued to wind sharply around timber that began to close in around them on all sides.

They finally came to a dead end sign and parked the car in front of a white, two-story house that loomed up from the forest before them. Jesse shut off the engine and they both sat looking up at the house.

The trees surrounding the house were tall. A huge sycamore dominated the yard. Behind the house smaller trees and dense brush were reclaiming what must have been an open field at one time. The sun was a deep crimson stain beyond the trees to the west. The windows of the house also reflected the blood-red hue of the sunset.

Jesse pulled the keys from the ignition and put them in his pocket. Jenna wondered if Abby would sense ghosts here. *She* sensed ghosts beyond those dark, vacant windows.

Now that she was here, this didn't seem like such a good idea. She wasn't sure if it was the house itself making her have second thoughts or if the idea of the Blackwells finding out that she had come up here made her feel so uneasy. It would be like stirring up a hornet's nest. Jesse was right. Technically, she was trespassing.

Her gaze swept the woods on her side of the car. She didn't know when she had ever seen such gloomy woods. A faint mist had begun to rise. Back in the deeper shadows of the timber was an outbuilding and alongside it an unpainted barn. The black doorway gaped wide with an almost menacing look to it.

Kane had told her that the barn had been filled with snakes when he was growing up and that his father wouldn't let anyone kill them. Most undisturbed old buildings harbored snakes. Black snakes that were six or seven feet long were not uncommon. Sometimes they hid in the rafters. Other times they nested in old hay. Jenna imagined there were snakes there now.

Kane had an almost obsessive fear of snakes. She had never seen anyone react to snakes the way that Kane did. He hated them with a passion.

"Looks like a good setting for a horror movie," Jesse remarked beside her.

Looking up at the house, she agreed. "I have heard some good ghost stories about this place actually." Still looking at the house, she said, "Try one of these brownies. They're really good."

Of course there would be ghost stories. The place looked haunted. Add to that the fact that an actual murder had taken place here, and you had a guarantee for spooky tales.

"You're right. These brownies *are* good," Jesse said.

"They're definitely worth a trip to the bakery. Even though it can be a little uncomfortable going in there. Irita Langston was the woman my ex-husband was having an affair with."

Jesse stared at her for a moment. "The bakery woman?"

"Yes." Jenna didn't comment further.

After a silence, Jesse asked, "So what are you looking for?"

She shook her head. "I'm not sure. Did you ever feel compelled to do something but you didn't know why?"

Jesse nodded. He definitely understood that feeling. Especially in his line of work.

Jenna knew one thing for certain. She was glad Jesse was with her. Now that she was actually here, she realized she wouldn't be able to go into that house by herself. Especially after dark. And it would be dark soon.

She looked at Jesse, who had just asked, "No one has lived here since the murder?"

"I don't think so. This was the original Blackwell home. When the cousins came, the family eventually moved into a bigger place with more room while Nolan, the brother who was killed, kept this place."

"You've got me curious now. Should we go see if the ghost stories are true?" Jesse asked.

"Uh huh," Jenna replied vaguely as she glanced again in the direction of the barn.

They opened their car doors at the same time. There probably wouldn't be any electricity, so she had brought a flashlight. A detail that Jesse had thought of as well. Feeling like Scully with Mulder in an episode of the X-Files, Jenna followed Jesse up the sidewalk leading to the house.

Tall weeds brushed against them, making Jenna wish that she had changed out of her high heels and skirt before she had come. Almost hidden in the weeds, an iron gate groaned on rusty hinges when Jesse pushed it open. She should have expected that. Gates and doors always creaked in haunted houses.

There was a huge stone slab that served as a step leading up to the front porch. They tried the knob on the door to see if it was open. It was locked.

They went around to the side of the house. In the deep shadows of the house the air felt even colder. There was another door there. And further back, towards the back of the house there was a cellar door with a padlock and chain on it.

After trying the side door, they were surprised to find it unlocked. Trespassing was one thing, but breaking and entering had definitely not been in her plans.

When the door had swung open a few inches, Jesse turned to her and asked, "Are you sure you want to do this?"

After her nod, Jesse pushed again and the door opened wide. Another slow creak disturbed the silence.

They went inside and found themselves standing in a narrow kitchen. A stale, musty odor immediately assailed them, a smell common to old houses, and probably made worse because of the lack of sunshine on this side of the house. It was darker inside but there was still enough light so that they didn't need their flashlights just yet.

Curtains still hung over the kitchen windows. They were drawn tightly as if to close off the kitchen from the outside world. A massive, built-in cupboard took up one corner. There were built-in shelves along one wall. Windows ran the entire length of the opposite wall.

A door to their right led to a small foyer. The walls were covered with wallpaper, a faded, old-fashioned print of green roses on pale green trellises. Halfway down the hallways, to the left, was a staircase which led up to the second floor.

The hallway led to the back of the house. There were two more rooms. A narrow parlor to the right and a tiny bedroom past the staircase.

In the parlor, Jenna stared up at the leaded glass windows and the embossed tin tiles that covered the high ceiling. There was an elaborate brass chandelier hanging in the middle of the room.

Most old abandoned houses were stripped of anything valuable. Not this one, however. Even though the antique fixtures and that tin ceiling alone would have been worth a small fortune.

There was heavy, dark woodwork throughout the house. The floors were all hardwood, too, although some rooms still had old carpeting covering part of the floors.

The kitchen opened to a small pantry at the back of the house. At the far end of the pantry was an unpainted wooden door that she assumed led to a basement. The door had an old wood locking device with a wood bar that slid into place. Most old houses had basements which were often used as root cellars. It wasn't uncommon to find snakes in basements, either. Not to mention spiders. Snakes she had no problem with. But spiders? That was a different story.

There was still some furniture in the house. Old pieces that were covered with dust and cobwebs. As Jenna followed Jesse back through the hallway and up the stairs, their footsteps echoed on the wood floors and gave back a hollow echo.

The bedrooms were mostly empty. The tall windows were dull with dust and most of them did not have curtains so there was more light upstairs.

What secrets did these rooms hold? Jenna wondered. What had it been like when people had lived here? She tried to imagine the sound of voices. Someone's dreams had gone into the building of this home. Children had grown and played here.

She didn't know what she was looking for, and she didn't know what she expected to find. There were no blood stains. Anywhere. There was an oval mirror hanging at the end of the hallway. It, too, was draped with cobwebs. Hanging between two doorways was an old picture depicting a violent hunting scene.

While Jesse searched through the other bedrooms, Jenna lingered in the small one he had just left. The low, sloped ceiling made the bedroom seem almost claustrophobic. A half-open door led to a closet.

Was this the room where the body had been hidden? She saw nothing to indicate that anything had happened here.

She heard a faint scratching in the corner of the wall. Probably a bird nesting somewhere in the eaves. It was such a tiny room, much smaller than all the others, and the only window was small as well. She stepped closer to see the outside view from up here and saw the barn with its black gaping doorway.

She still heard Jesse's footsteps, but it seemed she also heard something else from another part of the house. She listened carefully. The bird rustled again. Stopped. A tree limb rubbed against the side of the house. Or she imagined that it was a tree limb. That must have been the sound that she had heard. She could see the trees move from a slight wind. Did she imagine that the room was suddenly colder? Of course an old house would be drafty, she told herself. She shook off a sense of foreboding and depression.

But with the sensation of cooler air came the eerie feeling that something or someone was watching her. She glanced out at the barn again and could not suppress a slight shiver.

But she was not alone, she reminded herself. Jesse was with her. And suddenly she wanted to be with him.

She turned to leave the room. As she did so, she stepped closer to the closet. The door opened slowly on its own. It moved only a few inches but it was enough to startle her.

She froze but the door didn't move again. She leaned forward to cautiously look inside the dark closet. No skeletons. No ghosts. But there was an old trunk.

When she leaned her hand on the door frame and wondered what might be inside the old trunk, something crawled across her hand. She gave a little cry and jerked back, stepping straight into a cobweb that was hanging from the corner of the door. In a panic she pulled away and bumped her head on the edge of the door which was half closed behind her.

Jesse appeared a few seconds later. "Are you all right?"

She nodded but he continued to look concerned.

"I'm fine," she assured him. "I just stepped into a spider web and then I bumped my head on the door."

Jesse reached out to pull the sticky strands still clinging to her hair.

"There's no spider n my hair?" she asked hm.

He moved his flashlight over her. "No, not that I can see."

78

"There isn't one sitting on my back or my shoulder?" She turned for his inspection and finally released her breath in a sigh of relief and gave a little shudder.

He studied her for a moment. "You sure you're all right?"

"Yes. I just don't like spiders," she said.

"I found something," he said. "Come on. We're just about out of daylight."

She followed him to the last bedroom at the end of the hallway. There was an old iron bedstead in the room and a small nightstand beside it. There were curtains on the windows in this room. A carpet covered most of the wood floor. It was a rose-patterned carpet dulled by dust and time. Jesse's flashlight revealed what looked like a bloodstain on the floor in front of the closet. It darkened a portion of the carpet, as well.

He walked across the room and opened the closet door. "I would say this was where they found the body."

Jenna watched as Jesse examined the interior of the closet. After shining his flashlight all around inside the dark space, he said, "Nothing there. Thirteen years ago," he went on half to himself as he continued to examine the closet. "There wouldn't have been all the forensic tests that are available today. You have to wonder what was overlooked. Maybe some of your questions could have been answered."

He turned to her. "It would be interesting to run today's tests."

She nodded in agreement as he continued his inspection. Not only was it getting dark. The temperature was dropping, too. In spite of the jacket she was wearing, she couldn't suppress another shiver.

Turning back to her, Jesse noticed the shiver. "You sure you're all right?" he asked again.

"Yes," she answered. "It's getting cold and this place is beyond creepy."

"I agree," he said. "I feel it, too. Some places are like that. They make you feel like you need to be constantly looking over your shoulder. Want to have a look in the basement?" he asked.

With spiders and snakes down there in the dark? Not a chance.

She shook her head. "No, the sun is almost gone. Besides, I have run into as many spiders as I want to today."

He gave her a smile. "You're just thinking about egg foo young and egg rolls."

"You're right. I am getting hungry."

As they left the house and closed the door securely behind them, they were not aware of the pair of hostile eyes that were watching them from the darkness.

Chapter 10

Jenna set the table with a fresh linen tablecloth. She followed that with rose-patterned plates, her good ones. Napkins and silverware were next. In the middle of the table was a vase filled with a mixture of purple and white lilacs that were just beginning to open and fill the house with their heady fragrance.

While she was waiting for Jesse to show up with dinner, Jenna quickly straightened up the living room. She picked up several magazines and fluffed the pillows on the couch. No longer restricted by Kane's constant criticism, she had arranged the room just the way she liked it. From the pictures on the walls to the new sofa and chair she couldn't really afford but had splurged on anyway. When she saw headlights in the driveway, she opened the front door, expecting to see Jesse.

It wasn't Jesse, however. It was a very distraught-looking woman with a little boy in her arms. The child was crying and clinging desperately to the woman.

"I'm Amy Chambers, your neighbor," the woman gestured toward the nearest house. She was out of breath and trying to talk around the crying child. "I have been meaning to come over and introduce myself- "

"Is everything all right?" Jenna asked.

The woman shook her head. "No. I have to take my son to the hospital. I mean, my other son. He fell and hit his head. I don't have anyone to watch Devin. I hate to impose, but I don't know what else to do. Could you- "

"Of course." Jenna held the door wide open. "Come in."

The woman stepped inside. She had a large bag with her which she set on the floor. "There are bottles and diapers in the bag and a change of clothing for Devin. He's due for a bottle. It might help calm him down." She paused and brushed the gold-tinged curls off her son's face. "Oh, Dev. I know you don't want Mommy to leave you, but I'll be back as soon as I can."

She looked at Jenna. "I wouldn't leave him with just anybody, but I know you work at the police department and Beth Landen talks highly of you."

The woman turned to the window. "My husband is waiting in the car. I really have to hurry."

"Go," Jenna said, taking the child. "I'll take good care of him. I promise."

"I don't know how to thank you."

"Don't worry about it. That's what neighbors are for," Jenna assured her.

The disappearance of his mother behind the closing door was the signal for a round of ear-splitting screams and heart-rending cries for Mommy.

Jenna did all she could think of to quiet the boy down. She tried to feed him a bottle. She walked him around the house. She rocked him. She even tried to get him interested in the TV, but he was still crying and she didn't know what else to do.

She saw a second set of headlights in the driveway. With Devin in her arms, she opened the door to a surprised Jesse who was standing on the porch with two armfuls of paper bags.

"Where did he come from" Jesse asked as he walked to the kitchen and set the bags on the counter. He shrugged out of his leather jacket and listened as Jenna explained what had happened.

"I tried everything I could think of," she said. "But he's still crying. I don't know what else to do."

"If you want to get dinner ready, I'll hold him," Jesse offered and took the sobbing child from her.

Devin didn't take to the change of caretakers very well. He screamed out his unhappiness right into Jesse's ear. Jesse unpinned his badge and shifted the boy who continued to wail against his broad shoulder.

"Not sure what's going on, are you?" Jenna heard Jesse soothe softly as he walked the child from the kitchen to the living room.

"What's his name? Jesse asked from the other room.

82

"Devin."

"Hey, Devin. Everything's going to be okay." Jesse kept his voice low as he patted the boy's back.

He was a cute little boy with chestnut curls all over his head. Jenna guess that he was between one and two years old and was probably irresistible when he was in a better mood. At the moment, however, all Devin wanted was his mother.

She lost count of how many times Jesse walked the boy around the house, but it seemed to finally have worked. Devin was quiet at last.

Jenna peeked into the living room and saw that Devin and Jesse were both seated in her rocking chair watching a movie together. Devin had not yet fallen asleep. His little face was stained with tears and he was hiccupping softly, but he was snuggled tightly against Jesse's chest, clutching Jesse's tie in one fist. His thumb was in his mouth and he looked much more content than he had been half an hour ago.

Jenna had found a bottle of plum wine in one of the bags. She opened the bottle and poured wine into two glasses. She went into the living room and handed a glass to Jesse. They spoke quietly while Devin watched them with huge eyes, a little uncertain yet, but also a little curious now.

"I've never had plum wine before," Jenna said, sitting down on the couch. "I thought I would try just a taste right now and have the rest when Devin is gone."

Jesse took a sip from his own glass. "I thought you would like this better than sake, which is close to being the most godawful drink I have ever had. I had some once served at a Chinese place in Chicago. It's pretty potent stuff. Kind of reminds me of paint thinner."

She wondered what Jesse's life had been like in Chicago. She also found herself wondering about the women in his life and didn't like the strangely uncomfortable feeling that thought stirred up. Jesse had never been married. He had told her that himself. But had he left a woman behind? More than one woman?

"You have a way with children," she said.

"My aunts and uncles all had big families. I had a lot of cousins, so my first jobs were babysitting jobs."

"Really?"

He nodded. "So, yeah. I'm used to being around kids."

Jenna tilted her head, watching how comfortable he was with Devin.

"You're smiling," he said. "Does that surprise you?"

"No," she replied, the hint of a smile still lingering. "I just never saw you so domestic before.

"Domestic, huh?"

"Mostly I see you hunting bad guys," she said. "I'm not used to seeing you in the role of a domestic detective."

She had to say it twice to get it right, laughing at her efforts to say the tongue-twisting phrase.

"You're smiling now," she said as he leaned his dark head against the back of her rocking chair.

"Has it occurred to you," he said. "That every time we plan to have dinner together, we end up babysitting?"

"It does seem that way, doesn't it?"

Babysitting or not, Jesse was enjoying her company. He had never seen Jenna this relaxed. In his arms Devin gave a long, shuddering baby sigh. Jesse looked down to see that the boy had finally closed his eyes. He shifted the child carefully to make him more comfortable.

Soon after Devin had fallen asleep his father came to pick him up. The other child was going to be fine, they learned, but he was being kept overnight in the hospital for observation just to be on the safe side.

Dinner was still warm and waiting for them. Jenna talked about a garden as she spooned fried rice onto her plate. She found General Tso's chicken in another carton. Jesse handed her the egg foo young. She closed her eyes as she savored the first bite of an egg roll.

"This is so good."

Drawn by the soft, wistful quality in her voice, Jesse looked up from his own plate.

"I'll tell you a pathetic secret," she informed him. "I haven't had Chinese food since before my marriage. It was definitely too long a time to let that go on."

He wondered if she was talking about the marriage or the lack of Chinese food. Helplessly, he wondered what else she had been without for too long.

He was frowning as he set a carton of shrimp and lobster on the table before him. Don't think about the look in her eyes, he told himself. Or the way she just licked her bottom lip. He forced himself to drink calmly from his wine glass. Friendship, dammit. Remember you don't want to do anything to jeopardize your friendship with Jenna.

Lately he was surprised to realize just how important that friendship had become to him. They had spent a lot of time together these past couple of weeks. Not just at the office, but outside the office, too. He had helped her move. They had had lunch and pizza together. They had also made breakfast together after she had slept at his house.

He cut his thoughts short. He didn't need to be thinking about Jenna sleeping. In bed or on his couch. He was here for dinner and friendly conversation. That was all.

He would have only one glass of wine so that it didn't go to his head. He would act like a perfect gentleman, not some oversexed teenager ruled by a surplus of raging hormones. He reminded himself once again that it was a matter of willpower.

Yeah. Willpower. And he was doing alright. But he froze when she reached up to undo the clip holding back her hair. Those unruly curls had a habit of coming loose from the variety of female devices she wore to keep them tamed.

In spite of himself, her actions in coaxing the silky strands back into the clip seemed unreasonably erotic to him. Unreasonable, too, was the urge he had to wind his hand in those gold-tinged tresses and use them to draw her close and . . .

He blinked, completely at the mercy of a fantasy that involved her leaning over him with that long hair falling around him like a veil, those sultry eyes looking down at him with need and passion.

He shook his head. Egg roll, he told himself sternly. Try the damned egg rolls. And then she gave him another one of those smiles that seemed to play havoc with every one of his good intentions.

He cleared his throat and forced himself to concentrate on dinner. But his thoughts kept going back to Jenna. How could a man let her go? He wondered. If she had been his wife, he would have made sure she never wanted to leave him. He would have never given her reason to make her feel grateful that their marriage was a thing of the past..

"Did you have a close family?" he heard her ask.

"Pretty close. Yes. Relatively functional. And yours?" he asked, picking up his wine glass.

"I have two brothers and a sister. We were close when we were younger, but somehow we drifted apart over the years."

"You don't see them much?"

"No. Not much at all. Everyone is busy with their own families and their own lives." She was quiet for a moment, then added, "My father is getting remarried. I just got the invitation to the wedding."

There was a lost, almost sad look in her eyes for a moment before she said, "I guess he's not having any trouble moving on in life."

Jesse knew that Jenna's mother had died in a car accident several years ago. He gave her the opportunity to talk about it if she wanted to. She did talk about it, and about the drunk driver who had been responsible.

"I used to be so angry," she told him. "I used to think that it wasn't fair that he still had his family. He still had his wife and kids. I didn't realize what he was going through. About a year ago, he committed suicide. It was all so tragic. So many lives affected by one bad decision."

"I'm sorry, Jenna."

She shrugged. "I'm sorry, too."

She poured herself another glass of wine. Jesse pushed his glass forward for a refill, knowing that it wasn't a good move on his part. While they talked and drank the wine, he helped her clear the table and put the food away.

"We could watch a movie if you like, or just sit and do nothing and talk," Jenna said as she wiped the table clean. She paused, wondering if she was assuming too much. "Unless you need to get back home."

Jesse hesitated. Leaving would be the smart thing to do. But smart didn't seem to be at the top of his agenda tonight. He heard himself say, "No, I'm not in a hurry. Talking sounds good."

It wasn't good manners to eat and run, he told himself. Staying was the only polite thing to do.

They settled on the sofa in the living room. Jenna closed her eyes and leaned back, making herself comfortable. "No unpacking. No dinner to cook. This is like heaven. It's nice to sit down and relax for a change."

He agreed with her there. The murder investigation had been consuming a lot of his time lately. On his off hours, as much as possible, the subject was avoided. He had to step away from it sometimes.

"How are Abby and Josh doing?" she asked.

"They can't wait for you to bring those dogs home."

"I'm looking forward to it, too," she said. "We always had a dog when I was growing up." She put her stockinged feet up on the coffee table before her.

Jesse directed his gaze to the fireplace. "So wat else do you like?" he asked. "Besides dogs and Chinese food and exploring creepy old houses."

She thought for a moment. "Rainy nights," she said. "If I don't have to go outside." She closed her eyes. "The first snowfall of the year. The sound of wild geese returning in the spring. And you, Jesse?"

He turned his head to look at her.

"What do you like?" she asked.

You, honey.

He was surprised at how spontaneously that reply, and the endearment, came into his mind.

"I know you like peaches," she said.

"I do," he said. "And lately, sleeping in sounds real good," he said.

She smiled, in complete agreement with hm. "And you like to paint. What do you like to paint?"

"Horses. Landscapes. Wherever I find inspiration."

"Do you miss Chicago?"

"Sometimes late at night I find myself craving a good Italian beef or a Chicago hot dog and a cold beer."

She wondered what else he craved late at night. That thought had definitely come from the wine, Jenna told herself as she dared a glance up at him from beneath her lashes.

"But miss Chicago?" he went on. "I was raised in the country. I guess that stays with you. So, no, I don't miss the traffic or the crowds. And I definitely don't miss the crime. It never slowed down."

Jenna shifted her body and curled up into a more comfortable position on the sofa. Jesse still had his office clothes on but he had loosened his tie and his sleeves were rolled back, revealing very muscular, very masculine forearms. Why she found that so appealing was beyond her. She reminded herself that she didn't want to think of Jesse in that way.

"Some of my best memories are of growing up in the country," she told him.

"You grew up in the country?" he asked.

"Yes."

"I suppose you spent summer nights catching fireflies?"

She nodded. "And frogs." She pointed to her arm. "See this scar? I got this in a tree house."

He pulled his dark hair back to reveal a small scar on his forehead. "I got this one from a run in with a fence post."

As she leaned forward to see the scar, Jesse found himself suddenly fighting a completely impulsive gesture – a damned foolish one – to lean closer. To put his arms around her. To kiss her. His muscles tensed in the split second before he-

"Ouch."

Jenna suddenly leaned over and picked at the underside of the hem of her skirt. When she straightened, she was holding something between her thumb and forefinger.

"A sticktight," she said. "I have heard that these actually gave someone the idea for Velcro."

She dropped the tiny seed onto the coffee table. "I must have picked that up at the old house. And probably a few more that I haven't found yet." She flipped the hem of her skirt over, revealing a few more inches of shapely thigh.

Jesse waited until he was certain he could speak again without a catch in his voice. It was time to get out of there. Before he did something stupid. Before he did something they would both regret.

"We've both had a long day," he said. "And I have to get an early start in the morning."

After checking to make sure all the doors and windows were securely locked, he was saying goodnight and silently congratulating himself on his self-control.

He looked into the mirror and saw the woman's reflection. She was standing in the darkness behind him. She spoke to him but he couldn't hear her voice. He got an eerie feeling as he looked over his shoulder and saw that there was no woman behind him. Yet her reflection remained in the glass.

She was still telling him things that he could not hear. He knew he had to kill her or she would never leave him alone. He realized she was a witch and had power over him. And this terrified him.

As he watched in horror, she turned into a snake that slid smoothly along the rafters above him. The snake came closer to him and lowered until it was mere inches away from his face. It opened up its wide mouth, ready to devour him whole.

The dream shifted and he was looking down at the ground. He saw blood spattering. Slowly at first, like the first heavy drops of rain. Then here was a great deal of blood staining the ground and all that was on it. It kept falling, and the blood formed into words . . .

His eyes opened and he stared up into the darkness above him. As often happened after the dreams, the urge to kill was strong in him. It was even stronger later when his eyes swept the shadows and the doorways to the empty room, as if he was expecting to see ghosts in the moonlight.

He was seeing more and more all the time. Truths he had not known before. Revelations that made him understand more deeply.

He had once feared the darkness. Now the darkness was inside of him. There was power in yielding to the dark forces, in releasing the anger that had long been suppressed till it was like a coiled serpent. The darkness was an entity unto itself. He had not known that before, but he saw it clearly now.

He came here often, now that she was gone. He could move about freely in her absence.

He had watched her when she had not been aware of it. There was power in that, too. To find out who people really were, you had to uncover them in the darkness. When they thought no one was watching.

Chapter 11

Jenna drove an elbow toward her assailant's ribs, stopping just short of her target. At the same time she threw her right arm forward and broke her attacker's grip. She stepped back, waiting for the next move.

"That was very good," she heard Jesse say.

"Now, Jenna," he went on. "I want you to grab Abby in a front choke hold. Abby, show me how you are going to get out of it."

With a perfectly-executed downward swing of her arms, followed by a pretend knee strike, Abby was free of the choke hold.

"In this class you are going to learn how to defend yourself not only against punches," Jesse went on explaining. "But also against grabs and holds. Hopefully, you will never find yourself in a situation where you have to use any of these moves, but by the time you finish with these classes, you will know them. And you will be capable of successfully fending off an attacker. It doesn't matter what your size is or how big your attacker is. You can and you will learn how to take out any assailant."

There were over thirty women in the self-defense class which met for an hour and a half every Tuesday and Thursday night at the grade school gymnasium. Abby was there and she was already good at this because Jesse had been teaching her self-defense for some time now at home. She was an inspiration to the other women.

The recent murders apparently had the local women thinking about self-defense. And maybe, Jenna thought, some of them came because Jesse was teaching the class. A man as good looking as Jesse was bound to make the class more popular. Jesse definitely had their undivided attention at the moment.

"Now we're going to demonstrate what we call one-steps. They are defensive and offensive movements against an attacker. They are called one-steps because the person doing the attacking will be taking one step forward as you defend yourself. You will be working on three things. Balance, speed, and power. And don't forget to kiyep, ladies. I want to hear good strong kiyeps."

Jesse had already explained that the kiyep, or the yell, was important because it helped to free a person's inner strength or power.

"Jenna, you want to help me with this?" he asked.

Jenna stepped forward and stood facing Jesse.

"You're going to attack me first," he said. "Watch what I do. Then we'll switch places and you'll learn the defense part of it. Everyone else, get a partner. After we demonstrate, you are going to practice the movements yourself.

"When you are ready, Jenna, throw a punch."

Jesse easily blocked her. "All right," he said. "Now, let's do that again. I want you to hit harder and faster this time. Really try to attack me. I promise you're not going to hurt me."

Again, Jesse easily blocked her and immediately struck out with a sharp knife hand, stopping just short of her throat.

He went through another series of movements in slow motion. "Now you can see what the right move is capable of doing to an attacker," Jesse was saying to the class. "It has nothing to do with strength or muscle power. Jenna is much smaller than I am, yet she was able to easily throw me back. If she had pushed a little harder, she would have had me on the ground. Let's demonstrate that one again and then everyone can practice it on their own."

Jenna blocked Jesse's punch with her right arm. She spun around quickly so that her back was against his body. For a paralyzing moment she became acutely aware of the feel of his hard body molded against her own. She was supposed to be fighting him. At the moment, however, the only thing she was fighting was the urge to lean more closely into him.

"Now, drive your elbow towards my ribs. Like this," he corrected her and, taking her hand he turned her palm up. "You have more power this way."

"Do whatever you have to do to make me stop," he said closer to her ear this time. "All right, honey."

Was he aware of the endearment? She certainly was. It froze her in place. And was it her imagination or had his voice changed? It seemed huskier than usual and if melting her insides as one of Jesses goals in this lesson, then he was certainly dong a very good job of it.

Awareness raced through her veins like molten lava. Along with an intense rush of desire. Physical desire. No, that wasn't right. This was plain out and out lust.

"Now lock your right foot behind mine," she heard him say. "Turn your body and use both hands to push my shoulder back."

Jenna didn't dare look into his eyes. Concentrate, she told herself. But something had changed between them. Somewhere between his initial instructions and the execution of the movements, there was a shift in her equilibrium. She knew instinctively that he was feeling it, too.

Everyone is watching us, she reminded herself sternly as she felt the hard-muscled shoulder beneath her hands.

Jesse had been aware of the soft curve of Jenna's breasts beneath his forearm earlier, along with the warmth and scent of her body. They fit together perfectly. Too perfectly.

He could have sworn that she had leaned into him the slightest bit when her back had been against him. Then again, maybe he was the one who had been doing the leaning. It was the least of all he wanted to do to her. But not here. Not now. When she turned around, however, the dazed look in her eyes told him that she was feeling something, too.

While her one hand pushed against his shoulder, the fingers of the other hand curved against his chest. He said, "Don't hesitate, Jenna. Never hesitate." His voice was low and unintentionally intimate, his gaze not leaving hers.

It took Jesse a moment to discipline his thoughts. An entire class was watching them. They finished the demonstration, but Jesse was still frowning as he stepped away from her.

For the rest of the class he did not work with Jenna again. In fact, he barely acknowledged her presence at all. It was the only way he could get through it.

Jesse leaned over and opened the dryer door. He checked his shirt. It still wasn't dry. He put the shirt back in the dryer, shut the door and started it up again.

He walked over to the back door and leaned a forearm against the frame. He was shirtless and the sun was warm on his bare skin. He sighed and ran a hand through his still-damp hair as he listened to the quiet rhythm of the dryer.

He was losing his focus. He acknowledged that. The self-defense class last night had proven that to him. Just standing close to Jenna, he had experience a rush of desire so intense that it had thrown him completely off balance. And that wasn't good.

Right now what he needed to be doing was focusing all his attention of finding a killer, without having to deal with an over-the-edge sex drive which lately seemed to be stuck in overdrive. It was just a sex drive, wasn't it?

He walked into the kitchen and poured himself a glass of orange juice. He tossed the empty carton into the trash can. He would have to buy more when he went to town.

He walked back into the utility room and sighed, half in frustration, half in resignation. He was too old for this. But he found himself thinking about her a lot. She distracted him at the office, too. Leaning over a report together with her was enough to take his mind completely off work. Jenna had some kind of hypnotizing effect on him. As hard as he had tried, there was no denying it.

He realized the dryer had shut off. He pulled his shirt out, shook it out and shrugged into the still-warm sleeves. Even while he told himself that he should be giving Jenna some distance, he reminded himself that she still need the new locks put on her doors. He should have taken care of that already. And that mower belt wasn't going to last. The next time she tried to cut her grass, she was going to find herself with a mower that didn't work.

It was just a matter of helping her out, he told himself. Something he would do for any friend or neighbor. He would just stop by today, put the locks on her doors and a new belt on the mower. And then he would have all the time in the world for distance.

Of course, he also knew that if he was lying to himself this much, he was sinking a lot deeper than he ever imagined.

Chapter 12

Jenna pushed another stake into the loose soil. She had room for a few more tomato plants and some pepper plants. It would be nice to have some fresh potatoes, too. She had the room for them. She would pick up some seed potatoes when she went to town, deciding that it would be nice to be able to share the fruits of her garden with Jesse, Josh and Abby.

She sat back and brushed the dirt from her hands and found her thoughts returning to Jesse. Again.

She had told herself a hundred times that she didn't want a man in her life. She didn't want to be dependent on anyone else, emotionally or any other way. Dependency only led to disappointment.

So why was she thinking about Jesse so much lately? They were friends. Period. That's the way she wanted it to stay. Surely that was the way Jesse wanted things, too.

And yet here she was, sitting in the middle of her garden, acting like a silly teenager helplessly mooning over the man. She let her breath out in a deep sigh. She would just keep busy. That was the best way to stop thinking about him so much. Which was easier said than done, she realized, because once again she found herself going over that night in class and remembering how it had felt to be in his arms.

She groaned in frustration, shook her head and got up to water the new tomato plants. After the plants were thoroughly soaked, she went into the house to get a drink.

She washed the dirt off her hands and opened the refrigerator. Except for the white cartons of leftover Chinese food, the refrigerator was pathetically bare inside.

She poured the last of the orange juice from the carton and made a mental note to get more when she went to town. She tossed the empty container into the trash. She needed to pick up a bag of dog food, too, she reminded herself as a car pulled into the driveway.

She hadn't expected him this morning. It wasn't fair that the man looked like that. How could a faded blue shirt and a pair of well-worn jeans look so sexy? Easy, she immediately answered her own question. When they were wrapped around a body like that.

Through the kitchen window Jenna watched Jesse stop to play with the dogs in the yard. They were eating up the attention. The low, easy sound of his laughter drifted to her through the open window. A long sigh escaped her. She had no choice but to go out there and greet hm.

"Come on in," she said, pushing the screen door open. She turned away from him, taking a moment to recover from the major tremor that had rocked her from a brief look into his eyes.

"Morning."

The sound of his voice sent some pretty serious aftershocks through her, too.

"So," she said. "You've come looking for leftovers." She silently congratulated herself that she had managed to say it evenly enough.

"That does sound good," he said. "But actually I stopped at the hardware store and picked up some new locks and a belt for your mower. The one you have is shot. I'm surprised it's lasted as long as it has."

"Do you have time for all that?"

"Josh and some of his friends are getting paid to clean out an old barn. And Abby is at a friend's birthday party. So I have a few hours to kill."

A few hours? Jenna silently panicked. How was she going to survive a few hours alone with Jesse?

Jesse frowned. What the hell had he just said? A few *hours?* How did he think he was going to handle that?

He shifted his gaze and, still frowning, looked down at her palms. They were calloused from all the shoveling she had done that morning.

"Did you dig up your garden by hand?"

"Yes."

"I could have gotten a tiller and made it a lot easier for you."

She shrugged. "I didn't mind. It was a good workout. But I suppose I should have worn gardening gloves." She avoided those lethal eyes by looking down at her hands. "I'll pick some up when I go to town. I need some groceries anyway. The hardware store was supposed to get more plants in today."

"They did," Jesse told her. "I noticed when I got the belt." His frown suddenly deepened.

"What's wrong?" she asked.

"I forgot to get oil for the mower when I picked up the belt. But we can go to the hardware store together. No sense taking two vehicles. You can get your gloves and plants and I can get some oil. I wanted to pick up a new filter. I forgot that, too." Apparently, he could add forgetfulness to the growing list of things that had been afflicting him lately.

"But you have already been to the hardware store."

"It's only a ten minute drive, Jenna. It won't take that long."

"I have to do food shopping, too."

"No problem. We'll swing by the grocery store on the way back."

Jenna bit her lip. It wasn't going to be easy spending the next few hours with a man who made her insides do such strange things. And though it was against her better judgment, she heard herself say, "All right. But I need to change out of these dirty clothes."

Fifteen minutes later she came back downstairs in jeans and a lavender-blue top that bared about an inch of her midriff. She was also wearing a straw hat with a purple flower. All in all, Jesse thought, she looked damned irresistible.

I'm in some serious trouble here, he silently acknowledged to himself. Real serious trouble.

"You know," she said as she followed Jesse to his car. "I am perfectly capable of changing the oil in the mower by myself." He held the door open for her. She glanced up at him as she slid into the passenger seat. "And the filter."

She had always done those things herself. She had to or they wouldn't have gotten done. Kane had never found the time to do those chores for her.

"I'm sure you are more than capable," Jesse said as he settled into the driver's seat.

She gave him a sidelong glance. "I don't think of myself as a helpless female."

"Neither do I," He said as he fitted the key into the ignition.

"I have always done those things myself," she informed him.

"But have you ever put new locks on?"

"Well, no," she admitted. "But I could probably figure it out."

96

"Okay," Jesse said after he started the engine. "You are used to changing the oil in your mower. And the filter. You probably change the oil in your car yourself, too. And I have no doubt you would get the locks on. What I don't understand is why you are so uncomfortable having me help you with those things."

He was right. She was uncomfortable. It was hard for her to accept help of any kind. It always had been. "I'm not used to asking for help. I guess I don't like owing people," she admitted.

"I don't expect you to owe me. Anyway, you're not asking for help, Jenna. I'm offering it."

"Is there a difference?"

"Yeah," he said. "There's a difference."

Jenna leaned back in the passenger seat, trying to ignore how broad Jesse's shoulders were in the faded blue shirt. Or how the muscles in his forearms flexed as he turned the wheel. Or how in the blaze of early sunlight the blue shirt contrasted dramatically with his black hair. And how very sexy he looked when he put on a par of sunglasses.

"You know, Jenna, you have my permission to give me a good kick if I get too pushy."

He turned his face towards her, gave her a smile under the sunglasses and Jenna knew she was lost. Utterly and completely lost.

In Aker's hardware Store, Jenna fanned herself with her straw hat. The store was old, probably as old as the town itself. The floor was wood, worn smooth from years of use, and the displays were antiques. Some of the inventory must have been here for at least half a century. The store didn't have air conditioning and the sun was blazing through the front windows, raising the temperature to an almost uncomfortable degree.

The aisles were too narrow for carts. Jenna's sandals clicked on the wood floor as she walked over to where the shopping baskets were stacked, picked one up and slipped it over her bare arm.

She picked out some gardening gloves, blue ones with flowers on them, then exchanged them for purple ones that she liked better. She was aware of a few curious stares as she walked down the aisles with Jesse. A man in bib overalls, the hired help for the day, watched them as they passed. Two women shopping together gave Jesse more than a passing glance.

And why wouldn't they look? Jenna thought. *She* would look. A man as handsome as Jesse was bound to attract attention.

After reading the fine print on several boxes, Jesse threw an air filter into the basket. He followed that with some oil.

Jenna entered the cramped area where the seeds were kept. The sunlight falling through the front windows was bright and she adjusted the brim of her hat against the glare as she looked over the selection of seeds.

Jesse followed her and picked up a packet of seeds as he leaned against the shelf behind him. Right away he realized it was a bad idea. It brought him in close proximity to Jenna. Too close. Way too close. He tried to concentrate on reading the description on the seed packet he was holding, but he couldn't keep his gaze from straying over to Jenna.

The glow of sunlight was picking up the gold in her hair. She was biting her lower lip, deep in concentration as she made her selections. She was so close that he could smell the light, tantalizing scent of her perfume, close enough that he could feel the heat from her body. She was, he was thinking the most beautiful woman he had ever seen.

Focus, he told himself as he reached for another seed packet. "You would think they could find a better place to display these seeds," he said with a frown. "Isn't the heat bad for them?"

"It *is* a little crowded in here," she agreed. "And hot." She pulled her top out a little, fanning it against her body. "What are you looking for?" she asked, leaning over to read the package in his hand.

He froze when he felt the light brush of her arm against his. When he finally found his voice, he said, "I was supposed to get some seeds for Abby, although for the life of me, I can't remember what she wanted."

Remember? He was lucky if he could remember his own name at the moment.

"No idea?" She asked.

"No idea. Ab's good with any kind of flowers. Flowers and numbers. Any suggestions?"

"Well, first, are you planting them in sunshine or in shade?" she asked.

"Sunshine. Probably. Yeah, definitely sunshine."

"Any color preference?"

"Abby likes purple."

"So do I," she murmured as she looked over the seeds on the rack and picked up a package. "How about salvia? It will grow practically anywhere, sunshine or shade, and it's really beautiful."

Beautiful. He agreed. And she looked damned sexy in the hat, too.

"Of course, at this point, you would be better off buying the plants rather than the seeds."

"You think they have some outside?"

"They might." She lowered her voice to a whisper. "But they have a better selection at the grocery store. We could try there." She looked up at him.

All Jesse had to do was to lean a little forward, shift his posture the slightest bit, and he would be touching her body with his. It was a tempting thought. A thought so tantalizing that it refused to dislodge itself from his brain.

"Are you going to plant a vegetable garden, Jesse?"

The soft way she said his name momentarily had him tongue-tied.

"Might," he finally managed to reply. "Pansies."

"Pansies" he repeated at her questioning look. "That's what Abby wanted."

"I think," she said, leaning confidentially closer. "That I saw some pansies at the grocery store, too. But they like shade."

"Shade. That's- do-able."

As for Jenna, her reaction to Jesse was undergoing a purely physical shift. She couldn't help it. At the moment, she was aware of him on so many levels that her senses were absorbing him like rain in a parched desert.

"Ever grow them?" she heard him ask. "Abby wanted blue pansies."

Blue. Like Jesse's shirt. Covering that oh-so-male, mile-wide chest. She swallowed. Was it getting warmer?

"I never have," she managed to reply.

"What about salvia then?"

"Yes." She drew a deep breath as he reached out and slightly lifted the brim of her hat with one finger.

Without a word, she took the hat off and handed him a packet of seeds. "I bet Abby would like these. Moonflowers. She picked up an identical packet for herself. "They're one of my favorites. And their fragrance is- " She read the description and quoted, "'Intoxicating when they open at night.'"

"Intoxicating, huh?"

The low-drawled words stopped her. She stared at the words on the seed packet without really seeing them. She couldn't see them because she couldn't focus at the moment. All her attention was on Jesse.

And at that moment, down-right need was driving Jesse. He couldn't seem to think of anything else. He didn't want to think about anything else.

"They like- Oh." Jenna went still as she felt his hand lightly touch her jaw. "I think- " she breathed.

"Throw them in the basket," he whispered, leaning forward.

She felt his breath stir gently against the side of her neck. Time stood still. The world stopped spinning. She closed her eyes at the same moment that he kissed the side of her jaw. Lightly. Lovingly. Intoxicatingly.

"Jesse." Her voice was barely a whisper.

He tilted his face and leaned closer. With exquisite gentleness, his mouth grazed hers.

Jenna's hand, which had been resting against Jesse's chest, now slid up to his shoulder as the kiss deepened, became a long, slow, sensuous exploration.

Until a sound broke the spell.

Turning in the direction of Jesse's narrowed glance, Jenna froze when she saw the man standing in the aisle watching them. In an instant she took in the worn plaid shirt, the muddy boots, the mustache that matched the closely trimmed brown hair. And the smirk on Randal Blackwell's face.

There was something about the man's eyes that had always made her feel uncomfortable. Those eyes traveled the length of her body now, from her just-kissed lips down to her sandals. He made no attempt to hide his thoughts. It was as if he had reached out to physically violate her, and, as always, it made her skin crawl.

The smirk lingered in his eyes as he looked over his shoulder at the man in overalls. She saw them share a look. She knew how he would make this look. She knew, too, that by nightfall the story of how she and Jesse had been caught kissing would have already made the rounds of Alder Grove.

Jesse had stepped forward as if to shield her from the man. Jenna could not see Jesse's face, but she was instantly aware of a change in Randal's face. There was something sly in his eyes now that reminded her of a snake.

"Some people never heard of keeping it in the bedroom," he said.

A muffled snicker came from the man in overalls. Randal Blackwell had an audience. She knew it was something he thrived on. He looked back at Jenna.

"But I guess if you want to put on a display for the whole town, that's your business." He shrugged. "'Course, maybe she has a taste for big city detectives, and if she's willin' . . . "

Realizing that a scene here was only going to make matters worse, Jenna wanted nothing more than to leave the hardware store. But something told her that Jesse wasn't about to let it go. She was aware of the tensing of his shoulder muscles. She glanced down to see that his hand was closed into a fist.

Jesse's first impulse had been to wipe that smirk off the man's leering face. And he had nearly done so, but he felt Jenna's hand on his arm. "Let's just leave," she said in such in imploring voice that, after they made their purchases, that's just what they did.

Outside, Jesse turned to Jenna as she sat looking out the passenger window of his car. She remained silent for long moments. Jesse had wanted to protect her, but he felt like he hadn't done that. She was upset and she had good reason to be. And he didn't know what she was thinking right now about what had happened between them.

"You all right?" he asked, he words sounding woefully inadequate, even to him.

She was looking own at her hands. "I'm fine. I think it's best just to ignore the man. Randal Blackwell is a crude, arrogant bully. He likes to bait me. He always has. I think the best way to handle a man like that is to not give him the attention that he thinks he deserves."

Jesse sensed that there was more here that she wasn't saying. "What's he done, Jenna?"

Frowning, she let her breath out in a deep sigh as she stared straight ahead. She hadn't wanted to tell him, but she found herself doing just that. "During the divorce, Randal Blackwell threatened me with rape. He said he wanted to teach me a lesson."

"A lesson for *what* exactly?"

"For divorcing his brother. What you do to one Blackwell, you do to all of them, apparently."

Jesse's mouth tightened. His eyes took on a hardness she had never seen before.

"You reported it?" he asked in a voice that matched the look in his eyes.

"Yes. I told Dell. There is a report on file."

After a silence, Jesse said, "Hey, you know what? I forgot to grab those seeds."

He kept his voice light, but Jenna couldn't help but notice that the lightness did not reach his eyes. Those eyes were almost glacial as he left the car.

Jesse moved down the last aisle and faced Randal Blackwell. "You keep your distance from Jenna," he told the man.

"Is that an official warning?"

"It's a warning. It's as official as you want to make it," Jesse replied. "Your opinions are your opinions," Jesse went on. "But I'm telling you now that if you threaten or harass her in any way, you're going to regret that you even thought about it."

Jesse knew that Jenna hadn't wanted to cause a scene. He didn't blame her. But he didn't like men who bullied women around. He had faced a lot of them. And in the end, they all turned out to be cowards.

"You understand me?"

The man in overalls was watching with rapidly-shifting eyes.

"Yeah, I understand," Blackwell muttered, all the meanness of his nature oozing to the surface.

Jesse picked his change up from the scarred wooden counter and put it in his pocket. He picked up the small paper bag holding the seeds and put it in another pocket. He knew that Jenna was right. Keeping everything under control was probably the best thing here.

But he also knew that with an audience, Randal Blackwell needed to save face. He sure didn't like being told what to do. Anyone could see that.

"I'm not going to lose any sleep over what Jenna does," he said to Jesse's back. "Her business is her business. She can screw the whole town for all I care."

Yeah, Jesse told himself as he came to a dead stop. Control was the best way to handle the situation. On the other hand-

He spun around and grabbed the other man's shirt front. Without warning, he smashed his fist straight into Randal Blackwell's startled face.

Judging by the open-mouthed stares of the clerk and the handful of other customers, he knew he had just given the town something else to talk about, but at the moment, hell, he didn't give a damn.

Chapter 13

She had picked a fine time to find herself swept away by an earth-shattering kiss. In all her life, Jenna had never experienced anything like that. Nothing had even come close.

Somehow they had gotten through the rest of their shopping. Jesse had apologized for his behavior which he said had been way out of line.

They went back to her house and he spent the next hour or so working on her mower and putting the new locks on the doors. They didn't talk about the kiss again. She believed him when he said he had no intention of letting what had happened between them happen again. The problem was, why did that make her feel so disappointed?

As for Jesse hitting Randal Blackwell, right away there was speculation in town about whether the man was going to press charges against Jesse. So far he hadn't. But, of course there was talk. About the kiss and about the fight. Curiously, Jenna wasn't as concerned as she thought she would be. The truth was there was something about Jesse defending her that she found just a little bit chivalrous.

Two days later Jenna was standing out in the yard looking at the garden when the dogs began to bark. As she came around the side of the house, she saw the bed of a red pickup truck. So Kane had heard.

She mentally prepared herself for a confrontation as she stepped up onto the porch. Kane was already in the kitchen, which was something she was going to have to address. He couldn't just come into her house whenever he wanted to. His back was to her and his hands were braced on the counter as he leaned forward. Not a good sign where Kane was concerned.

He turned slowly. One look at his face made her dread what was coming. Not too many people saw this side of Kane. He normally kept darker side hidden. Except from her.

The dogs were barking at him through the screen door as he questioned her. "Where did you get those mutts?"

"At the pound," she answered.

His mouth straightened into an unpleasant line. "What are you going to do with two dogs?"

"What do you think I'm supposed to do with them?"

Aside from the hunting variety, Kane didn't have any use for dogs. And these two apparently didn't like him, either. They continued to bark. They growled. They scratched at the door. Things they never did with Jesse.

"Shut up, Kane snarled in their direction.

"They are only doing their job," she told him.

"Their job?" he echoed. "If you mean their job is being a damned nuisance."

"They aren't to me." Jenna spoke a command and the barking gradually ceased, but the dogs still seemed agitated.

"I suppose you don't mind drool and shedding all over the porch, either. And cleaning up after- "

Max, the bigger dog, gagged like he had just eaten grass. After some loud retching, he finally spat out a mouthful of vomit that did, in fact, contain grass.

Kane stared at the dog for a moment longer, then turned and glowered in her direction.

"It's late, Kane. What do you want?"

He didn't answer her right away.

"What do you want?" she repeated wearily. She wasn't up for his games right now.

"I want an answer as to why you were up at the old house."

He had caught her a little off balance with that question. She wondered who had seen her there. With Jesse.

"Whose idea was it to go up there?" he wanted to know. "Yours or your boyfriend's?"

"It was my idea."

"There are no trespassing signs up, you know."

He was staring at her with narrowed eyes when he asked abruptly, "Did you find it?"

"Find what?"

"What you were looking for."

"What would I be looking for? It's an empty house."

"That's right," he said. "It's an empty house, so I don't know what you expected to find."

A tense silence dragged on.

"I wouldn't have expected it of you," she heard.

"Expected what?"

"You lying to me."

"What are you talking about?"

"About you and him being just friends."

"I didn't lie."

"Really. Well, it's all over town about your little display at the hardware store."

She had always hated the way he changed everything that went on between a man and a woman into something vulgar. He was doing it now. His mouth twisted into a sneer.

"I'm not going to stand here and discuss gossip with you," she informed him.

"So how long has it been going on?" He asked as his eyes continued to bore into hers.

"How long has what been going on?"

"Simple. How long has he been fucking you?"

He had gone too far. "I want you to leave. Now."

They had fought a lot during their short marriage. There were times when she had seen Kane lose control. Times when he had broken things in anger, but his violence had never been physically directed towards her. Right now, however, his hands were clenched into tight fists at his sides. It looked as if the rage inside him was about to explode.

She reached for the doorknob, about to open the door and tell him again to leave. He reached his own hand out and slammed the door so hard that the house shook with the impact. He leaned forward and placed his hand flat against the wall next to her.

"Don't play games with me," he said through his teeth.

"I'm sure it's hard for you to believe," she said, forcing herself to look straight at him. "But every interaction between a man and a woman does not always have to do with sex."

He gave an ugly little laugh and, when she tried to turn away, he grabbed her chin roughly. "What do you think your detective boyfriend wants with you?" Something mean flared in his eyes before he jerked his hand away from her chin. "He just may surprise you before the last body turns up."

That alarmed her. "What do you mean by that?"

"You don't find it just a little too much of a coincidence that a woman turns up dead only after he shows up here? We never had anything like this before he came. That first murder was never solved. He's always first on the scene. He knows about forensics. From what I hear, the killer knows how to clean up and not leave any clues behind. Do you even know anything about his past? Does anyone?"

Jenna was appalled by his accusations. Of course, she didn't believe him, but if Kane repeated those things to enough people, it could cause trouble. Jealousy had often motivated Kane in the past. She knew it was motivating him now.

He watched her face closely, smugly believing, she knew, that he had put doubts about Jesse in her mind. And then, abruptly, as he had done so many times during their marriage, having to have the last word, Kane walked out, leaving her standing alone in the kitchen.

She watched to make sure that he locked the gate behind him. Then she made sure the kitchen door was locked. Something she would see to from now on. Then, still standing with her back against the door, she stared across the room at her stack of notes about the murders. They were still on the counter where she had left them.

Jesse was sitting in a corner booth with Sheriff Wade and Deputy Prichard at the diner. They were just finishing lunch. It had been a long morning. They had spent hours setting up an emergency detour around a bridge that had washed out.

"Hell of a downpour," Bear commented as he looked out at the gray curtain of rain outside the window.

The rain was loud on the roof, nearly drowning out the clatter of dishes being cleared from the tables. Most of the lunch crowd had already left the diner, but some people were standing by the front doors, waiting the heaviest rain out.

Lightning crackled, a little too close for comfort. It was followed by a deep rumble of thunder that rattled the window panes of the diner. People stepped back from the windows. Bear remarked that they reminded him of a coop full of nervous hens with a fox outside.

"I thought the rain was supposed to let up by noon," Bear said before he drained his coffee cup.

"They got this one wrong," the sheriff remarked.

The rain had, in fact, ended several times, the sky even clearing to blue patches more than once that morning. But as soon as it cleared up, more clouds would roll in and it would start raining again.

The waitress approached the booth and began refilling their coffee cups. "You order this rain, Bear?" she asked.

"Hardly," was Bear's reply. "It'll be at least another week before my fields even begin to dry out."

"More coffee, sheriff?" she asked.

He silently pushed his cup forward.

"Got any cherry pie left today?" Bear asked the waitress.

"Got pie for you, Bear," she replied.

"I'll have some pie when you get time, Maris," Bear said as he tore open another packet of sugar and added it to his coffee.

After the waitress left to get the pie, Bear said in a lowered voce, "I think you're right, Jesse. Cyril Clayton coming up missing after he discovers the body of a murder victim is just a little too coincidental."

In addition to the two murders, there were now two unsolved disappearances. No leads on either case, and no way to know for certain if they were, in fact, related.

In Jesse's interview with Cyril Clayton's wife, the woman had told him that after a night of heavy drinking, her husband had hinted that he 'knew something' but that he also knew how to keep a secret.

"Right now," Jesse sighed. "I'd welcome any leads."

"I wouldn't even know where to begin to look for Blue," Bear said. "He hunted everywhere. And he wasn't in the habit of telling anyone where he was going or when he would be back. That covers a lot of territory. And you've got to wonder where the dog is."

"What's the Blue stand for?" Jesse asked.

"Cyril had one blue eye and one brown," Bear said as he hunched over his coffee cup and cradled it with both hands. He was thoughtful as he watched the crowd that was still bunched around the front doors.

"I don't know what's going on with dogs around here lately," he said. "Tanner Lanning's got one missing. Not only that, but I talked to Joe Dunn this morning. His dog showed up on their back porch with an arrow through its neck. That was the same night Joe thought he saw someone watching the house from the woods. Hard to believe, but the dog's all right."

Dell said, "Could have been a hunter."

"Could have been," Bear commented as the waitress set a plate of cherry pie before him. They watched as the waitress disappeared behind the counter.

Bear picked up his fork. "Everything that's happening around here has got everyone spooked. People are starting to worry about each other. They don't know who to trust any more. Not their neighbors, apparently." He shook his head and picked up a bite of pie.

It was true. They had gotten a lot of calls, a good portion of them anonymous, about suspicious activity or outright accusations about who the murderer was. They had to check every one of those calls out.

"Scare people enough and they'll start turning on each other," Dell said. "Things are probably going to get a lot worse before they get better."

"H'm," Bear muttered nodding in agreement as he took another bite of pie.

The sheriff's cell phone rang.

"Yeah." He listened to the voice on the other end, then asked, "Dead or alive? Uh huh. We'll meet you up there."

The sheriff ended the call, flipped his phone shut and put it back in his pocket. "Found the dog."

The rain had finally ended. At least for the time being. The clouds were dissipating once again, yielding to patches of bright blue that covered most of the sky. Violets were purple splashes of color among the brown of last year's leaves.

As the men tramped through the soggy weeds, one of the deputies already on the scene approached the three officers who had just arrived. The deputy sidestepped to avoid a low area filled with rainwater.

"Been a hell of a lot of ran these past few days," the deputy said. "There's Jessup over there," he said, pointing. "He was out with his kid mushroom hunting when they saw the buzzards. Then they found the dog."

"Did they move the dog?" Jesse asked.

"No."

"Good. Let's have a look at it."

"We've looked around," the deputy went on as they trekked over towards the trees. "We haven't turned up anything yet. Just the dog."

The men reached the place where the dog had been found. The dog was half hidden by a fallen, moss-covered log. A quick examination of the body revealed bullet holes. Two of them.

"You're sure it's Blue's dog?" Jesse asked.

"Yeah, I'm sure. Blue used to drive around everywhere with that dog in the back of his pickup truck. That's why Jessup called in to report what he'd found. Everyone knows that Blue is missing."

Bear, who was a dog lover, was down on his heels beside the dog. He got to his feet. His hands were clenched into fists at his sides. "Why in the hell would someone have done this?"

"You think there's more to see here?" the sheriff asked. They all knew what he meant.

"That's a definite possibility," Jesse replied, his gaze taking in the surrounding woods. His gut instincts had been kicking into high gear since they had arrived.

"Okay, men. You all know what we're looking for," Sheriff Wade said to the men. "Take your time and try not to disturb anything. This whole place might be a crime scene."

The men fanned out in a line and searched the woods. After an hour of searching they had found nothing.

"There's just nothing here," one of the deputies said.

Bear, with his hands on his hips, was studying the lay of the land. "Isn't this where the old Bowden house used to be?"

"I think you're right, Bear," the sheriff said. "There's a clump if irises growing over there."

Irises didn't grow wild and were a good indication that a house had once stood on a particular site.

There was a shout.

"That was close," one of the deputies said, panting as the other men reached hm. "Too damned close."

"What happened?"

"There must be an old well there. I almost fell through. I heard the boards cracking just before my boot broke through. I stepped off to the side at the last second."

The rest of the men approached and gathered around the old boards. The grass was fresh and green beneath the broken pieces of wood.

"These boards are old but they haven't been here very long," the sheriff said, getting down to inspect the ground closely. He pushed the spongy, half rotted boards aside.

110

"There's something down there," the sheriff said grimly.

The men standing around the well looked at each other. From the depths of the rock-lined hole rose the tell-tale odor of decomposing flesh.

Chapter 14

Two days after the bodies of Cyril Clayton and his dog were found, Jesse as in the office staring out the big windows that overlooked the town square. Behind him the long table was covered with forensics reports, autopsy findings and every other kind of report pertaining to a murder investigation.

He had put in long hours sifting through every piece of evidence, looking for something that might have been overlooked. He believed that the same person who had committed the murders of the two women was also responsible for the murder of Cyril Clayton whose body had been recovered from the abandoned well.

Yesterday a forensics team had arrived from Springfield. They had spent all the rest of the day processing the area around the well for clues. The crime scene was virtually clean. Which led him to think that the killer had some knowledge of forensics because he knew how to clean up so well. Well enough that minimal evidence was left behind.

Of course, there were enough books and TV shows to give anyone a rudimentary education in forensics. Not to mention the internet. But Jesse also knew that you couldn't operate like this indefinitely and not leave something behind.

The rains weren't helping. It was possible, likely, that evidence had been washed away. The newspapers were reporting the worst flooding in nearly sixty years. Bridges were closed. Crops in low-lying areas were lost. And portions of some country roads were completely under water.

Jesse turned back to the room and stared at the papers and the notes strewn across the table. There as something there. A key to solving the crimes. He just had to find it.

The report on the gravel mixture found on both victim's bodies had come back. It was a mixture of mortar and creek gravel, which had commonly been used in building foundations for homes in the area. Since it had been used for at least a century, there were probably hundreds, maybe thousands, of homes built with that kind of foundation.

Jana Calder's autopsy report had indicated that she had fallen down a flight of stairs. Jesse's guess was that the victims were being kept in a basement for a period of time before they were killed. It was an important piece of the puzzle, but all the pieces weren't together yet.

Forensic analysis and technology was one thing. It caught the majority of criminals. But in a closed society like Alder Grove, Jesse had a gut feeling that the human element was going to play a major role in finding the killer.

Somewhere out there was a human predator with a thirst for blood. He hunted prey because he liked doing it. Jesse's years on the streets of Chicago had shown him what kinds of things human beings were capable of doing to each other and it wasn't a pretty picture.

Jana Calder's stabbing had been brutal, up close and personal. As savage as the first attacks were, however, Jesse knew that the perpetrator would become even more violent. His fantasy was building along with his confidence. He was evolving.

Jesse narrowed his gaze beyond the windows. He killer had spent a lifetime developing a mask that he hid behind. He was able to be sociable when he wanted to be. He had developed the ability to get his victims to trust him. People knew him. Probably liked him. He shopped in the same stores, ate at the same restaurants, attended the same functions. But he also had a darker side. Cyril Clayton probably knew him for what he was. Maybe there were others who knew, too.

One thing was certain. He had to be stopped. He wouldn't stop killing until he was caught.

Jesse massaged the back of his neck. He would probably work well into the night. Again. It was almost 1:00 and he hadn't taken a lunch break yet. Dell was late. The third time this week. Some trouble at home that he had hinted at, but didn't go into. Bear had worked the late shift last night. He wasn't due to come in till 2:00.

The door opened. It was one of the task force members back early from lunch. The man was tall and solidly built, younger than most of the other team members. He was a hard worker and he knew his way around a crime scene.

He greeted Jesse, pulled a chair up to the table, and gathered the reports he had started working on early that morning. "Is the secretary back yet?" he asked.

Jesse looked over at the man. "No," he replied.

Jenna would be gone running errands most of the afternoon.

"I thought if she had the time, I might have her help me get these papers in order," the man said.

After a silence, Jesse heard, "She's not married. Do you know if she's dating anyone?"

Jesse frowned and replied after a few moments, "You would have to ask her."

"If she doesn't want you on the property," Jesse heard Bear say in the outer office. "Then you're going to have to stay away."

Jesse glanced up at the clock and realized that Bear had come in early.

"But my things are still there. What am I supposed to do? Can I at least call her?"

"Not until the court date," Bear answered. "You can't have any contact with her at all. If you try to talk to her and I find out about it, I'll have to pick you up."

Bear was good at maintaining control in domestic disputes, but the argument was heating up.

"I'm supposed to stay out of my own house?" Jesse heard. "That's bullshit and you know it."

Jesse caught a glimpse of the man as he leaned over the desk. "I'm supposed to stay away from my own wife? Just because you say so?" he went on.

Jesse stepped to the doorway.

"Not because I say so." Bear tapped the badge on his chest. "But because this gives me all the authority I need to bring you in if you assault or harass your wife again."

In the ensuing silence, Jesse heard Bear breath a deep sigh. "Look. I understand how you feel, Jord. But she's asked the court for protection and whether you like it or not, you're going to have to back off and do what she says. Until the court date."

"Yeah, until the court date." The man muttered something under his breath that Jesse couldn't catch. The door banged loudly behind him as he left the court house.

"There have been a lot of domestic calls lately," Jesse commented as he walked into the room.

"There have," Bear agreed. "I think I've seen more calls in the past few weeks than I saw in the last five years."

There had been a dramatic rise in reports on domestic disputes. And domestic disputes, they all knew, had the potential to be some of the most violent. There was a shrill creak as Bear settled back in his swivel chair.

"Smells like a Christmas tree in here," Jesse said.

"I trimmed some pine trees for my mother," Bear said. "They were getting hard to mow around. I must have gotten sap on my clothes. I got it all over my hands." He held his hands out before him. "It's almost impossible to wash that stuff off."

"How did your domestic battery call last night go?" Jesse asked. "Anybody get hurt?"

"Someone got hurt, all right," Bear chuckled. "Christa Krupp has been taking self-defense classes from you. She thought her husband was a prowler. She flipped him right off the porch. We thought he had a broken leg, but it turned out to be just a sprain. Guess Chuck will think twice before he tries to sneak in the house after a night of heavy drinking."

Bear got up and poured himself a cup of coffee, grimacing after his first sip. "When's the last time this coffeepot was cleaned out?"

"Bob made the coffee. Jenna's been out most of the day," Jesse told him.

Bear nodded as if that explained it. He settled back into his chair. "You've been putting in a lot of hours lately. Any new ideas about who it is we're dealing with?"

Jesse shook his head. "No hard evidence right now."

They spent some time discussing the latest domestic cases, but nothing stood out that would specifically lead to a suspect.

"So, does this profiling really point you to a killer?" Bear asked.

"It points us in the right direction," Jesse replied.

"It's hard to think anyone could be capable of the things this guy is capable of."

Jesse nodded, agreeing with him. "What can you tell me about Randal Blackwell?"

"Randal Blackwell," Bear repeated, leaning back in his chair and rubbing his chin. "I went to school with him. He's always tried to maintain a tough-guy image, but mostly I think he's all talk."

"Any actual assaults on record?"

"No, but Jenna filed a report on him a while back." He told Jesse about the details of the report. "Other than that we don't have anything on him. Oh, I'm not saying that he can't be a mean sonofabitch. And the threats he made against Jenna were way out of line."

"What about Jenna's ex-husband?" Jesse asked.

"Kane? He was a few years younger than I was. A bully wannabe in school. Didn't stand out much. He's got a temper, been in a few bar fights. But like his brother, nothing we ever pulled him in for."

"What about the murder thirteen years ago?" Jesse questioned. "Do you know anything about that?"

"I haven't thought about that in a long time," Bear replied. "Terrible thing. Shocked everybody around here. I had just joined the force then."

"I heard there was a lot of animosity n the family."

"Animosity?" Bear scoffed. "Hell, it was pure out and out hatred." He took another sip of his coffee. "A lot of bad blood there. The cousin who did the killing was mean. Made life hell for all those kids for a long time."

"Know why he would be talking about revenge?"

Bear shrugged. "I sure don't." A frown settled on his face and he pursed his lips thoughtfully before he said, "You know I was wrong about Kane not having anything in his past. There was an incident way back. If I remember right, he had gotten a girl drunk once and lured her into the woods. I don't know any of the details of what happened but she was pretty shaken up. She never did press charges though."

Bear finished the coffee in his cup and said to Jesse, "You'd better take your lunch break now. I've got a hunch that with the fourth of July coming up we'll be even busier around here than we are now."

Chapter 15

Jesse had been in the office for only half an hour when the call came in about another body. He drove his Jeep across a muddy field and met Bear who was already on the scene.

Bear was spattered with mud. His uniform trousers were wet to his thighs.

"She's over there." Bear pointed across the wide, fast-running creek.

Jesse looked in the direction Bear indicated. His gaze narrowed as he followed the sweep of leaves and the tell-tale debris that marked the highest point of the flood.

No one had to speculate on what had probably happened. Heavier rains than usual had washed this latest body out of some hiding place along the creek. Maybe from a shallow grave. The flood water had tremendous force and would flush out everything in its path. It even toppled huge trees and boulders and washed them down the creek. The killer hadn't taken into account that they were experiencing the worst flooding in more than half a century. Jesse followed Bear to the creek bank.

"Normally the creek here is shallow enough to walk across," Bear said. "Easy. It even dries up completely in the heat of summer. But running as hard as it has these past few days- " His voice trailed off as he stepped carefully into the water. Ignoring the mud and the high water, Jesse waded across the creek with Bear.

The badly decomposed remains were caught in the partially exposed roots of a massive tree growing alongside the creek. The remains were so badly decomposed that an ID was going to be difficult.

It was a gruesome discovery. Particularly gruesome because there was still rotting flesh hanging from the corpse. The unmistakable smell of death hung on the air.

"Who did you say found the remains?" Jesse wanted to know, carefully navigating the slippery rocks on the creek bottom as he worked his way closer to the body.

"A guy out hunting the creek for arrowheads," Bear informed him. "The floods wash them to the surface and make them easier to see."

"The guy still here?"

"He's over there," the deputy pointed. "He's pretty shook up over it. He's not a local. He's from out of state here visiting his brother."

The body, or what was left of it, was lying partially in the water. It was almost definitely female because of the long hair. She was lying on her back with a slight tilt to the side. One arm was caught in a tangle of tree roots. The arm was raised as if it was pointing to something overhead.

The area was so remote it was a wonder that the body had been found at all. It was within view of a very old, long-abandoned farmhouse set back at a distance from the creek. The front porch and part of the roof of the farmhouse had collapsed.

Jesse frowned as he noted the color of the hair. It was muddy, but the water had washed part of it clean where the current caught it. The sun suddenly came out and the hair glinted with a golden tinge where it trailed in the water. There, at least, a pattern was emerging. All the victims had a similar hair color.

"She's been here a while," Bear said. He grimaced and corrected himself. "I mean, she's been *somewhere* out here for a while."

"Yeah," Jesse agreed, still frowning as he continued with his cursory examination of the body.

She had washed out of a shallow grave maybe. Or a cave. Carved out by the water over thousands of years, caves were pocketed into the rocks everywhere above the usual flood lines. If it hadn't been for the floods, the victim might never have been discovered.

"We don't know the cause of death yet," Bear said. "She might not even be- "

"No," Jesse said, straightening. "This is our guy." He stared down at the body. "It looks like she was shot. That might be the cause of death. We won't know for sure until we have an autopsy done. An ID is going to take some time."

The force of the water on the decomposing flesh was going to make everything difficult. Very difficult.

"We don't want anything in the area disturbed until the team gets here," Jesse said. "But we want to get her out of the water as soon as we can."

"We haven't touched to body," Bear assured him.

"That's good," Jesse said.

Bear, who had been staring at the body, suddenly looked away. "Sorry, I- " he began. "I haven't got much of a stomach for this."

"None of us do," Jesse said. "But we don't have any choice but to try and stay focused."

"I know you've dealt with this a lot," Bear said in a low voice. "But I don't think for me there could be any getting used to it. I don't ever want to get used to it. I don't know how in the hell anyone could get used to this."

"Maybe you need some time to- " Jesse began.

"No," Bear interrupted him. "Hell, we need to do everything we can to catch this bastard."

"We need to get this area processed as soon as possible," Jesse told him. "The creek is changing by the minute. And if we get more rain, it's going to make things even harder," he said as one of the other deputies approached.

"There's no rain in the forecast," the deputy said.

"Forecasts can be wrong," Jesse said almost absently as he scanned the area. "They've been wrong more than once this week."

"This is where the body washed up," Jesse went on. "But evidence could have washed anywhere. We'll have the team search up and down the creek."

It wasn't going to be easy. The creek wound in and out through the entire county and beyond, splitting off into small tributaries and pools everywhere. Not only that, but the course of the creek was changing constantly.

Bear was watching Jesse who turned to look at the body again. The mouth was open as if in a silent scream. The gold hair was tangled in the tree roots. On the arm pointing up was a bracelet. If they were lucky, it would help with an ID.

This victim's hair was longer than Keara Eland's. But that thought didn't give him much comfort. She was somebody's daughter.

"We're going to do everything we can to find out who she is," Jesse said. "She deserves a name."

He knew that nothing was insignificant when tracking down a killer. Anything might become a crucial part of the investigation.

"I didn't see any shoes," Jesse remarked half to himself.

"What did you say?" Bear asked as he turned to him.

"Her shoes. I don't see any."

"I don't know," Bear said. "Part of her is in the water."

"She's barefoot," Jesse informed him. "Her shoes might have been washed away by the force of the water. But it's also possible she's one who got away. If that's the case, she might have something important to tell us."

"What makes you think that?" Bear wanted to know.

"Just a hunch," Jesse replied. A hunch and the fact that she was still wearing a bracelet. That bracelet would have been too irresistible a souvenir for the killer not to have taken.

"A search of the creek isn't going to be easy," Bear commented as he looked in the direction of the first sharp bend which was only about twenty-five feet away.

"I agree," Jesse nodded. "It's going to be a hell of a job. But we can start with whatever is caught on that piece of fence over there."

Bear pivoted around and saw what he had not noticed before. At the edge of the flood-swept field above them, something was caught in the uppermost, sagging strands of barbed wire that bordered the field. They didn't know exactly what it was but it was plainly more than normal leaf debris.

Chapter 16

The discovery of the body, complete with all the gory details, made the front page of the newspaper. It had been determined that the remains were of a female between the ages of fifteen and twenty-five. No ID yet. They were going to try to identify her by her teeth or the bracelet. Jesse thought that the bracelet was a better bet.

A gunshot wound had been the cause of death. The material caught in the barbed wire fence had definitely come from the victim. They still had found no shoes. If they were out there, they could be anywhere. They could even be buried in the mud somewhere. A task team had been working round the clock, combing the creek for several miles upstream and down and every accessible area near it. So far, they had turned up nothing.

The victim's feet, or what was left of them, showed signs of deep cuts and lacerations. A piece of glass had been embedded deeply into one foot. Traces of smoke, specifically kerosene smoke meant that the glass had come from a kerosene lantern, which supported Jesse's theory that the victims were being kept in a basement.

Jesse tossed a folder onto the long table before him, impatient for that ID. He was waiting to learn the time of death, or as close as they could determine. Time was a crucial factor.

He crossed his arms over his chest and looked up at the board that held the pictures of the three known victims. All the women were in the same age group. Their hair color was approximately the same. And those facts bothered him. Jenna fit the same description.

He had gone over pages of detailed forensic analysis again and again. He arranged and rearranged the known facts in his mind, trying to make the evidence add up to solid answers. A pattern was emerging with regard to the victims, but it wasn't enough. He still didn't know how the perp was choosing his victims. Or why.

These women represented something to the killer. Calia Devoss and Jana Calder had both come from well-to-do families. It was possible the killer had a hatred of people in a higher social class. Not unusual. Death was one way to level social status. They had found no other connections in the women's backgrounds, however. No other similarities. Except for the hair color

One thing Jesse was certain of. Being on the front page of the newspaper was giving the killer the power and attention he craved. He enjoyed having people think he was scary. It was another form of control.

Jesse narrowed his eyes, his gaze intent on the board in front of him. He had gone over everything so many times that he was finding it easier and easier to get into the killer's mind.

He was learning, perfecting his method of killing. It had become an obsession for him. At first he had used a gun. Stabbing was much more intimate. He wanted to watch his victims die up close. He wanted his face to be the last thing they saw.

There was no rain and none in the forecast. They sky was a deep, cloudless blue through the openings in the trees. Jenna had looked forward to a long walk in the fresh air. She needed time alone to think, to sort things out. The office was chaos lately. The investigation never slowed down.

The pine trees behind her home gave her a beautiful place to walk. With the sun filtering down through the fringed canopy of trees, the woods took on a peaceful, almost surreal atmosphere.

She paused and drew in a deep breath of the morning air. She felt as if she had reawakened in some strange, inexplicable way. To nature. To herself. Something had changed her. Jesse's kiss had changed her, she realized.

She didn't know what to do with these new feelings. She had vowed to keep them to herself, but it was getting harder to do that. Every day with Jesse seemed to pull her more deeply into- Into what, she didn't know.

She stopped her thoughts short leaned over and reached to pick up the disc of gold glittering on the mat of brown pine needles. She suddenly jerked her hand back, pulled out her cell phone and called Jesse.

Jesse was there in fifteen minutes. He had brought Abby with him. While Abby played with the dogs in the yard, Jesse questioned Jenna about the earring.

"How long has it been missing?"

"I'm not sure. A few weeks."

"Have you noticed anything else out of place?" he asked. "Have you been missing other things?"

"Yes," she said, frowning. "Small things. Things I thought I had misplaced because of moving. I thought they would eventually turn up."

"Like what?"

"A stationary box. Jewelry. And I have looked everywhere, but I can't find one of my nightgowns."

She didn't like the look in Jesse's eyes.

"I was missing my keys for a while," she told him. "They weren't gone for long. Just two days."

"Just long enough for someone to make duplicates," he said.

"You think someone has been in my house?"

"Let's err on the side of caution and say that it's a possibility."

He looked around at the woods. "The pines are thick up there. They look nice, but they're a perfect screen for someone who might want to watch you. You stay here. I'm going to have a look around."

He climbed the wooded hill behind the house and disappeared into the woods. Then he checked every door and window of the house.

"If there were any footprints besides yours," he said when he had finished. "The rain has washed them away."

He had brushed up against the trees. The smell of pine was strong on his clothes.

"I want you to think carefully, Jenna. Have you noticed anything unusual lately? Even something that seems insignificant."

"There is something else."

His face grew even more sober as she told him about the hold in the door at the other house.

"I don't know how that earring got out there, Jenna, but after what you just told me, we need to consider the possibility- " He corrected himself. "The probability that someone has been watching you. Is it possible your ex-husband could be stalking you?"

"I wouldn't think so," she replied. "But I suppose anything is possible."

"And Randal Blackwell has threatened you," Jesse said, frowning. "It's not going to do you any good for me to tell you that I'm sure nothing is wrong. We've got three dead women. Another one who is missing. And a possible witness who might have been killed by the same person. There is a murderer loose out there." He paused while he drew a deep breath. "I want you to consider staying with me for a while."

A long silence passed before she said, "But I just moved here."

A very serious-looking Jesse said, It's the only way that I'll feel you're safe, Jenna. You're too isolated here."

"I appreciate you wanting to look after me, but do you really think we should do that?"

"Look, Jenna," he said, lowering his voice. "What happened between us in the hardware store has nothing to do with my asking you to come stay with me. If someone has been watching you, they might have already been in the house, too. Until we have some answers, I don't want you staying alone."

"But imposing on you like that- "

"Who said anything about imposing? A live-in cook and babysitter will come in handy."

Jenna knew he was trying to lighten the gravity of the situation. But what they were talking about was a big change. A very big change. For both of them.

Jesse knew he hadn't completely convinced her yet. "The only way I'm going to be able to sleep at night is if I know you're safe. Do you really want to be responsible for my sleepless nights?"

"But what about the dogs?"

"We'll take the dogs with us."

She half relented. "I suppose I could be ready tomorrow."

"No. Now, Jenna. We'll help you get whatever you need for the night."

"People will talk."

"I don't give a damn what people might say. Do you?"

She shook her head. "No."

"There's plenty of room for you. I've got a bedroom and a study empty. You can have your pick."

He went quiet and straightened. Abby had come out onto the porch. She was holding Tasha, the female dog, in her arms. "Is Jenna going to come stay with us?" Abby asked, her face lighting up at the thought.

Jesse looked at Jenna, waiting for her answer.

"Yes, Abby," she said quietly. "I'll come."

Chapter 17

Jesse wasn't about to take any chances with Jenna's safety. He had worried about her living alone all along. Finding the earring in the woods and hearing about the hole in the door had only made him more determined to keep her with him.

He had the team check out her house and the surrounding woods. Other than the earring and the missing items, there were no signs of an intruder. That didn't mean someone hadn't been in her house or that someone wasn't watching her.

Signs of voyeurism were definitely present. And he couldn't ignore that. Voyeurism might start out as a passive act, but he had known it to turn deadly. Secretly spying on women when they weren't aware could involve violent fantasies that had the potential to escalate to murder.

Her ex-husband might be involved. Bear had mentioned an incident with Kane Blackwell years ago. So far, Jesse hadn't been able to dig up a report that would have given him details. It seemed the information was missing from the files.

He had found out, from more than one source, that Kane Blackwell was still territorial where Jenna was concerned and that he wanted her back. The man wasn't going to like the idea of her moving in here with him.

It might be difficult for Kane Blackwell to think of his ex-wife living with another man. But it turned out that it was even more difficult for Jesse.

They had discussed arrangements and he agreed with Jenna that they would deal with things on an adult level. Two days went by and it was working out fine. Until the third morning.

A half-naked, dripping wet Jesse had bumped into Jenna coming out of the utility room.

"Sorry, he said, taking a step back. "We were out of towels in the downstairs bathroom." He took another step backwards.

"Abby used them to give the dogs baths last night," Jenna told him.

The ends of Jesse's black hair were dripping. Drops of water were clinging to the lean angle of his freshly-shaven jaw and his muscular shoulders and chest.

For several long moments they both remained frozen. A split second later they were in each other's arms, kissing as if their lives depended on it.

"Jesse, wait," Jenna panted. Leaning back against the wall behind her, she held her hands out before her as if she could hold him off that way.

"You're right," Jesse managed in a husky voice. "We agreed. We'd . . . keep things under control."

Staring up at his face, into the eyes where passion still smoldered, Jenna tore her gaze away, down to his bare chest, and to the flat, sculpted abs, and lower to . . .

"I'll just, uh, I'll get some towels. And let you get ready for work," she said before she quickly turned and fled.

There were five men seated around the small table. They were drinking coffee and talking as they did every morning.

"She washed up near the old Metz place," one of the men said. "Heard she was half skeleton."

The gas station door opened, and they greeted the man who had just come in. He got himself a cup of coffee and joined the others, sliding into the last remaining seat at the table.

A copy of the latest newspaper was on the table, surrounded by coffee cups, donuts and empty sugar packets. The headline, in bold, attention-drawing letters, gave a five-word summary of the murder. The rest of the page gave the details.

"Hell of a deal," one of the men commented, nodding at the paper before him.

The newcomer took a careful sip of his steaming coffee. "I don't know what the world is coming to. Have they identified the body yet?" he asked.

"No," another man replied. "Not someone from around here. There's no one missing from the county."

They talked about the flooding, and about Hollis Sheer's new tractor, and how the price of feed was getting out of hand. Their talk centered around local news. Every one of them was a life-time resident of Alder Grove. Anything beyond the county limits seemed foreign and suspicious to them.

The last man to take a seat at the table offered his own opinions on the usual subjects. He laughed at the private jokes, shared the latest gossip and offered to help one of the men fix the starter on his truck.

For a moment the article on the front page of the newspaper held his attention. He looked down at the grainy photograph accompanying the article. It showed the location where the body had been found.

She had washed a long way downstream, he thought to himself. A long way.

He recalled how she had knocked over the lantern, shattering glass everywhere. Spilled kerosene had spread the fire. She could have burned the house down.

He had gotten so mad that he had hit her hard. Hard enough to knock her unconscious. At least he thought she was unconscious. While he had been putting out the fire, she had gotten away. Ran right up the steps and out of the house.

He had grabbed his gun, got off one shot and thought he had hit her. He had always been a good shot. He had had a lot of practice at it. It was dark, however, and he had trouble tracking her. He had spent hours searching but she had vanished into the darkness like a ghost.

The following days had been a tense period for him, not knowing if she was alive or dead. Or whether she would show up somewhere and tell what he had done. He had hoped and prayed that she was dead. Months passed and he knew that she would probably never be found. It was even possible that wild animals had torn her to unrecognizable pieces. He could only hope that was the case.

He looked up, laughed at a ribald joke one of the men had made about a woman passing by on the street outside. Then he picked up a donut and settled back to watch the morning traffic.

Jesse set his keys on the counter. He loosened his tie and pulled it free. With a sigh, he stretched, working out some of the kinks that had become routine for him.

It had been another long day. These days he usually stayed late at the office. Sometimes everyone else was in bed by the time he got home. Things were probably better that way. Less time around Jenna meant less chance for a repeat of the other morning.

Tonight he was home relatively early. He had missed dinner but he could smell something good baking in the oven. Abby came into the kitchen

"What smells so good?" he asked her.

"There's a peach pie in the oven," Abby said. "Jenna helped me make it."

"Well, it smells really good, Abby. Where is she?" Jesse asked, trying to keep the question as casual as possible as he got dinner out for himself.

"Taking a bath upstairs."

He nodded, sitting down with a plate of food. "Did you teach the dogs any new tricks today?" he asked.

Abby giggled. "Tasha can roll over now."

Between bites of roast beef, Jesse said, "I'll bet you'll have her jumping through flaming hoops by the end of the week."

Abby was good with animals. Tasha would do anything for her. Both dogs had taken well to the move. They were already inseparable with Josh and Abby.

Jesse buttered a thick slice of homemade bread. "Looks like someone was busy cooking today. Did you help make the bread, too?"

Abby nodded.

"This is a very good dinner," he said to her.

"If you marry Jenna, she could cook good dinners for us forever."

Jesse's fork stopped halfway to his mouth. He didn't say anything. He didn't know what to say.

Things were getting complicated. As it stood now, both he and Jenna went about their day pretending as if nothing had happened between them. As if the kiss – the *kisses* – had never happened. But sometimes things got awkward. Sometimes he didn't know what to say or how to act around her. So he tried to avoid her.

After he finished dinner, he cleaned up his dirty dishes and then stood alone in the middle of the empty kitchen. He was folding a dish towel when he heard her come down the stairs. She didn't come into the kitchen. He heard the screen door to the front porch open and close.

He hung the dish towel back up and wondered what to do next. The truth was he liked coming home to a house with Jenna in it. She really took pleasure in preparing meals and taking care of the family. He had not failed to notice that Abby was doing a lot better with Jenna here. Jenna watched TV with both kids. She played games with them. She baked them batches of brownies and homemade cookies. It was damned nice having her here. It didn't make any sense pretending different.

He was still telling himself that after he poured some of her hand-squeezed strawberry lemonade into a glass and walked out onto the porch.

Jenna, with Abby nestled beside her, was using one foot to slowly rock the porch swing back and forth. They were reading, each one with their own book. Jenna looked up and smiled when Jesse sat down in one of the porch chairs. As if she was happy to see him. A warmth stirred low in his belly, a warmth that wouldn't go away. And the truth was, he didn't want it to go away.

Despite his inner reaction to her, he managed to say calmly, "That was a good dinner, Jenna."

"You'll have to thank Abby, too. We'll have pie in a little while. It's peach. Abby made it all by herself."

"I know. She told me."

"You like peach pie, Uncle Jesse," Abby said. "You ate almost all the pie the last time Jenna made one."

"Guilty as charged," he confessed. "I'm a glutton for peach pie."

Jenna gave a little laugh. "We'll have to make two pies the next time."

She looked like she belonged here on his front porch. The sunlight was shimmering off her gold hair. She had fluffy pink socks on. Abby had matching ones.

"You girls are going to spoil me with all this good home cooking."

"We like spoiling you, don't we Abby?" Jenna said as she looked over at him.

Jenna, too, felt a warmth seep through her. It always did when they were together. The late afternoon sunlight touched Jesse's dark hair with a golden brush. It lit up one shoulder and the bare forearm resting on the arm of his chair.

Jesse, half frowning with his silent thoughts, tried to make sense out of what was happening to him. He knew what he wanted. He had kissed her. Twice. He wanted to kiss her again. He knew what she tasted like. He knew how her body felt against his. Those were things a man couldn't easily forget.

The truth was that right now what he wanted more than anything else was to pick her up and carry her upstairs to his bed. And after that, he wanted to make love to her. Deep, passionate love that would banish the bad memories her ex-husband had left her with.

Jesse had seen the way men looked at her at work. He wasn't blind to the way they turned to stare at her on the street. He wanted her to notice him. Not ex-husbands. Not task force team members. He wanted her to think about him the way he was thinking about her right now.

He blinked once as he tried to re-direct his focus, then looked at Abby who had just asked Jenna a question.

He asked his own question. "So what is it you two are planning now?"

"We're doing pedicures later," Jenna answered him.

"Pedicures, huh." He sat back in his chair, listening while they talked about colors of nail polish and wondering how in the hell he was going to make it through another week.

He got up from the bed in the darkness and pulled his clothes on. She probably wouldn't like that he was leaving in the middle of the night without saying a word. But it didn't matter to him what she thought. She knew what she was getting herself into.

Hell, she knew what she was doing. She had known back when he had first taken her into the woods during his birthday party. She had liked it well enough to let it happen again.

She'd had a lot to drink. Enough that she probably wouldn't wake up for hours. It was less complicated that way. Half a bottle of whiskey and some rough sex had satisfied her and had taken the edge off his needs for a while, but now that those distractions were gone, he was feeling the anger creeping up again. Just how far did he have to go, he wondered?

Taking care of Blue had been one thing. Blue's body being found was another stroke of bad luck, of which there seemed to be plenty to go around lately. The details of the murders were leaking out and a lot more questions were being asked. And those questions could lead right back to him, some of them.

He scowled and tilted the bottle of whiskey up to his mouth then drained another inch or so. The welcoming fire blossomed in his belly as he looked down at the woman lying on the bed.

Kane had bragged about getting her into bed so he knew it would be easy. He continued to look down as he buckled his belt over his soft white belly and wondered if something would have to be done about her. She meant nothing to him. She was just a convenience. She wasn't all that good-looking. And she could stand to lose a few pounds.

He wondered if she needed to be up early to open the bakery. But that was her problem, he thought as she snored quietly. It didn't matter to him one way or another if she made it to work on time.

Women. They all seemed to work these days. That hadn't been the case twenty years ago. Women stayed home. They knew their place and expected to take care of things there.

That got him to thinking about Jenna. Another working woman. From the very day she had moved here, Jenna had thought she was better than any of them. She wasn't though. She was just a whore like every other woman he had ever known. But he thought about her. A lot. Lately his fantasies seemed to revolve around her. Last night he had even imagined for a while that it was Jenna that he was pounding into.

His mouth twisted. Mr. Jesse Logan was going to be a problem. His features grew hard with hate. He would show that bastard. He would get back at the sonofabitch if it was the last thing he ever did.

He would show Jenna, too. Women were all the same. You couldn't trust a one of them. There was a lot of satisfaction in knocking them down to a level where they knew their place. There was even more satisfaction in imagining Jenna personally getting her payback. Yeah, paybacks were hell.

Women, he thought bitterly, were behind all the troubles in the world. Somewhere along the line, all problems led back to a woman.

He had never realized that as much as when he had buried the pocket knife that Blue had given him. Buried it so deep that it would never be found.

Chapter 18

"No, I am not going to spend the rest of the day in bed."

Jenna wasn't quite sure how to deal with Jesse. At the moment he was acting like a very difficult, very stubborn child.

"Well, all right," she said, setting the tray on the bed. "It's your decision. But at least consider having breakfast in bed since I've gone to the trouble of bringing it to you."

"I can do that," he relented, picking up a piece of bacon from the plate on the tray.

During last night's self-defense class, Jensine Larch, a large woman, taller than Jesse and outweighing him by more than a few pounds, had taken his instructions a little too seriously. While he was teaching her how to escape from a rear bear hug, Jensine had stomped on Jesse's foot with over two hundred pounds of determined woman behind it.

"It's just a small broken bone in my foot," Jesse continued to argue. "It barely hurts."

"That's because you have been resting it all night. Walking around on it is going to make it feel much worse than it does now. I can guarantee it, Jesse."

He lifted a dark brow in her direction and saw one corner of her moth twitch the slightest bit though she was doing her best to hide it.

"It wasn't funny, Jenna," Jesse informed her.

She was biting her lip now, trying hard to keep any trace of humor from showing in her face.

"All right. Maybe it was a little funny," he conceded. He pointed his fork in her direction. "But it wasn't that funny."

Just then Josh interrupted them. He was carrying a big vase overflowing with flowers. He handed Jenna a card then set the vase on the dresser.

"How sweet," Jenna said as she read the card. "The flowers are from Jensine Larch. She's very sorry about last night. This is really nice of her. I'll bet these flowers are from her yard."

Jensine had one of the prettiest yards in town. That wasn't all. Josh informed them that there was an angel food cake downstairs. And a pie. Cherry.

There are some thank you cards in the desk downstairs," Jesse said. "I'll send one to her. Lord knows, the woman feels bad enough."

"How about a pain pill?" Jenna suggested.

"I probably won't even need one," Jesse said as he sat on the edge of the bed and slowly stood, carefully testing his weight on the injured foot. Jenna continued to watch him.

"All right," he growled. "Give me a pain pill."

His cell phone rang. Jenna watched him flip it open.

"Damn," she heard him say under his breath. He closed the phone and put it back in his pocket. "We have to get to the courthouse. Now."

It was chaos in the courthouse. People crowded the various offices and the hallways. They were even standing on the front steps. Reporters were firing questions everywhere.

Jesse walked up to Bear who said, "It's crazy in here. It's been this way since word got out that there's another missing girl."

"You can't keep a thing like this contained," Jesse said and asked, "Where's Dell?"

"Up trying to secure the scene."

"Where exactly is the scene?" Jesse wanted to know.

"West of Buck Ridge," Bear replied.

Jesse's lips compressed for a moment. The woods went on for miles up there. There would be a lot of ground to cover.

"Where's the girl," he asked.

"In the Record's Room," Bear answered.

"Clear out the back room and put the girl in there," Jesse told Bear. "And then, except for the task force, get these other people out of here. Put them outside in the park if you have to. Just make sure to keep everyone out of the conference room. Lock the door if that's the only way."

The Alder Grove Police Station wasn't set up for this kind of thing. Jesse glanced across the room one more time. A muscle at the side of his jaw jumped as the task force member who had shown an interest in Jenna brought her a cup of coffee. No. It wouldn't be coffee. She didn't drink coffee. It had to be tea. He must have made it especially for her.

"It looks like half the town's in here already," Jesse muttered. "We'll probably have the rest of it in here by noon."

Bear took off his hat long enough to run his hand through his hair. "We also have press here from every major city within fifty miles. What do you want us to tell them?"

Harlan from the local paper approached the two men. "Is it true that you have someone in custody? That there's a suspect?"

Another voice asked, "Who is it? Someone from around here? Is it a cop?"

Jesse looked sharply at Bear, who informed Jesse in a low voice that there was, in fact, a suspect in custody. "He was picked up less than an hour ago."

Bear went on to say that the suspect had been sitting in his car at the rest stop outside of Raynard, the next town. He had blood on his clothes and was being held in the Raynard jail.

"The girl said that the guy used a badge," Bear told him soberly.

"Did they find a badge on the suspect?"

Bear shrugged. "I don't know anything about that."

Jesse frowned and nodded thoughtfully. Reporters crowding the doorway shot another question at him. What's the name of the missing girl?"

"We can't give out that information at this time," Jesse replied. "Right now you have to let us do our job. We'll let you know of any developments as soon as we can."

By the time Jesse had finished talking to the reporters, Bear had already moved the girl to the back room. Miraculously, no one had noticed.

"If you think it's crazy in here, you should see the crime scene," Bear said as they stood outside the door to the back room. People have taken it upon themselves to search for the girl. Everyone and his brother are out there wanting to help."

Not good, Jesse thought to himself. It meant probable contamination of the crime scene. Which meant their job was going to be a lot more complicated.

"Give me a brief description of what happened," he said to Bear.

"About midnight last night, I responded to a call about a disturbance at the Muddy Alley. I'm dealing with two drunks outside the bar when I get another call about an assault on two girls up by Buck Ridge. Around 12:45 I raced out to the scene. I found the girl's vehicle off to the side of the road. First thing I did was to make sure the area was secured. Then I went up to Tom Ellard's place. His wife had called in about the girls.

"We've already rounded up nearly a dozen deputies to comb the woods up there. They've been at it for the past hour. They haven't turned up anything yet."

"Call up to Hillyer," Jesse told the deputy. "A man named Holt up there trains search dogs. See if he can bring a couple of his dogs down here. And I want the name of every single person that volunteers to help or anyone who shows an interest in the crime scene. When I'm through here, I'll have you take me to where the vehicle was found and see what we can find up there."

"You think this could be a cop?" Bear asked.

"Anything is possible," Jesse replied. "But, no," he added grimly. "I think it's more likely that he's gotten a hold of my missing badge."

"Felicia Morris?" Jesse asked as he opened the door to the back room. "I'm Detective Logan. I know you have been over this already, but if you could tell me what happened to you last night, it will help us catch the man responsible."

The girl was visibly shaken. Her jeans were muddy. There were cuts and scratches on her face and hands. Jesse also noticed bruises on her throat. She had obviously been through a traumatic experience.

"We had borrowed a friend's car," Felicia began. "We were going to Keara's house to tell her mother that she was all right. With all that has been going on, Keara was worried that her mother would think that something bad had happened to her."

Jesse looked hard at the girl for several moments before he asked, "Your friend was Keara Eland?"

"Yes."

Felicia paused, her expression bleak as if it was painful for her to recall all that had happened. "The car got a flat tire," she went on. "I couldn't get a signal on my cell phone. We were out in the middle of nowhere so we were going to try and change the tire ourselves. We were still sitting in the car when another car pulled up behind us."

"Can you tell me what kind of car it was?" Jesse asked.

"No. All we could see were bright lights. He kept the lights on even when he came up to my window. He said he was an off-duty police officer and that he would help us. But then he started acting differently. He said he was going to have to search the car for drugs or alcohol. He kept shining his flashlight in my eyes, so that I couldn't see him. Then he told us to get out of the car. We were scared. We were afraid of what would happen if we didn't do what he told us to."

"Did you see his face?" Jesse wanted to know.

She shook her head. "No. He kept blinding me with his flashlight. But he was tall. And he had dark hair." Although she had never clearly seen his face, she explained that she had gotten a glimpse of his back in the mirror as he was handcuffing Keara.

She stopped. Her eyes closed before she drew a shaky breath and went on. "Everythng happened fast after that. I didn't have time to think. He made us both lean against the car. He put handcuffs on Keara. He tied my hands behind me with duct tape. That's when I knew something was wrong.

"He made us walk with him into the woods." Felicia covered her face with her hands and she began to cry. "He took Keara somewhere else into the woods and told me to stay where I was. When he came back, he- He didn't say a word. He put his hands around my neck and squeezed. He kept choking me until I must have passed out. When I woke up, I was lying on the ground. I didn't see the man anywhere. My hands were still tied behind my back, but I was able to pull my hands under my body so that my hands were in front of me. I got up and ran. I didn't stop to try and free my hands. I just ran.

"I couldn't get the tape loose and it was hard running like that in the dark woods. Then I remembered I had a mirror in my back pocket. I broke the mirror and used it to cut the duct tape."

"What happened to the duct tape?" Jesse asked.

"I threw it in the woods and kept running. When I got to a road, I followed it to the first house I saw. The people there called 911. Then *he* came." She looked up at Bear.

The girl's wrists were raw where they had been taped. Her hands trembled badly as she twisted them in her lap.

"Did he use anything besides his hands on your neck?" Jesse asked as he gently inspected the bruises.

She shook her head. "No."

In his office, Jesse closed the door behind him and said to Bear, "We need to get the girl to the hospital to be checked out. The bruises need to be documented and her clothes will have to be gone over for trace. After we get things under control here, we'll go up to the crime scene, then we'll go talk to that suspect over in the Raynard jail."

Jesse wondered if Felicia Morris knew how lucky she was to be alive and safe. Keara Eland wasn't so lucky, however. She was still out there and he knew that time was running out.

In the outer office, a deputy came up to him and said, "We called the missing girl's mother. She's here."

Celeste Crayden stood in the doorway. She was alone. Her whole body was rigid as she searched the room. Terror and dread were written all over her face as her gaze connected with Jesse's.

Jesse walked up to the woman and took her arm gently, guiding her away from the reporters. "Mrs. Crayden, why don't you come into my office."

Raynard was an even smaller town than Alder Grove. After receiving a call from the Raynard Police Department, Jesse decided to interview the suspect there before going out to the crime scene.

A deputy met them in the parking lot outside the Raynard Police Station. After brief introductions, Jesse learned that the arresting officer was still inside with the prisoner.

"That was fast work," Bear commented.

"Maybe too fast," the deputy returned. He wavered a moment then said, "Doesn't make much sense."

"What doesn't?" Jesse asked.

"That he would be hanging around afterwards, just sitting in a rest stop. You would think he would be long gone."

Jesse agreed with the man, but he kept his thoughts to himself.

The deputy shuffled one foot and frowned as he went on. "He's banged up some."

At Jesse's raised eyebrows, the deputy explained, "You'll have to listen to the guy's story."

Jesse did listen. He saw right away that the man had none of the physical characteristics that Felicia Morris had described. He was shorter for one thing. And he had red hair that was thinning on top.

"Let him go," Jesse said after a brief interview. "He's not the one we're looking for."

The arresting officer was seated in a swivel chair behind a desk. He was a heavyset man with a bald head and he didn't like what Jesse was saying.

"But he's a stranger," the officer began to protest.

"Being a stranger isn't a crime," Jesse told the man.

The chair gave out a loud squeak as the officer stood.

"Neither is being parked at a rest stop," Jesse said, his gaze fixed on the man before him. "He's not the guy we're after," he repeated.

"Oh," the officer leaned forward over the desk. "You can tell just like that?"

"Yeah," Jesse replied, holding the other man's gaze. "Just like that."

The officer wasn't convinced. He folded his arms over his chest. "How can you be so sure?"

"Because I've been trained to know."

"What about the blood?" the officer wanted to know. His chin lifted. His jaw tightened.

"He got a nosebleed from hitting his nose on the car door when he was dragged from his vehicle," Jesse replied.

The officer straightened. "That wasn't from me. I drove up just as he was being pulled from his car by some guys that had heard about the missing girl."

"Technically, that could be called assault," Jesse said. "At this point, what you need to do is to give him a formal apology. It wouldn't hurt to throw in a meal and a tankful of gas. Then hope like hell he doesn't press charges or decide to sue the town."

Chapter 19

Checking out the suspect had wasted valuable time. Time they didn't have. Jesse was impatient to get back to Alder Grove.

"So," Bear asked after a long silence as they drove. How do you really know he wasn't the right guy?"

"For one," Jesse began. "He has an alibi. Four hours ago he was sleeping in a hotel room in Wilstown. He used a credit card to pay for his room and his breakfast at 8:00 this morning. That won't take long to check out. They should have taken care of that already."

"H'm." Bear checked his rear view mirror. "So what else makes you so sure?"

"He didn't fit the physical description. And I didn't see any indication that he was lying," was Jesse's reply.

"You always know when a man is lying?"

"Most of the time," Jesse replied, frowning at the woods alongside the road. "That and he didn't fit the profile."

"That profiling stuff really works?" Bear queried.

"Yeah, it works."

They passed the sign that said: ALDER GROVE, 5 MILES AHEAD, then Bear turned left onto a gravel road. Still thinking over what Jesse had said, he made another noncommittal grunt.

"Besides," Jesse said. "It's someone from around here. A local."

Bear glanced sharply at Jesse. "What makes you so sure?"

"Because he knows his way around the woods. A stranger would have been noticed. He has access to a basement. He knows where to hide bodies. He thinks about it, plans it out well ahead of time stalks his victims. He's also getting more confident. He'll kill closer to home. And he's following some kind of personal agenda."

Bear nodded thoughtfully, his face sober and his lips set in a thin line.

Jesse was thinking about something else he didn't want to have to face. He was thinking about that badge. You could get anything over the internet these days. Of course, in the dark to a scared teenage girl, even a plastic badge might look real.

But it was more likely that it was his missing badge. Which wasn't good. The last place he remembered having it was when he took it off at Jenna's house. The night they had had Chinese. He had taken it off when he had been holding Devin.

If the killer had his badge, it could mean only one thing. He had been in Jenna's house. It was the only place he could have found it. The frown deepened on Jesse's face as Bear drove past Vidia Blackwell's house.

The field behind the house was littered with all kinds of junk. An open space behind a dilapidated, sagging barn was also filled with old cars, trucks and broken machinery. There were refrigerators, lawn mowers and who knew what else rusting in the weeds.

"An eyesore, isn't it?" Bear remarked as they passed the house.

Jesse agreed, but he didn't comment.

"I don't know why anyone would want to save so much junk," Bear said beside him "Doesn't bother them, I guess. Collecting junk started with the old man. He took anything he could get his hands on and dragged it here. It reminds me of squirrels stashing away nuts for the winter. They think they might need it someday. Maybe being poor had something to do with it."

Jesse had studied the problem of hoarding. He knew that it was a sign of a deeper psychological problem. People held onto worthless objects with the belief that they were more valuable than they actually were. Sometimes they developed deep sentimental attachments to useless items. It provided a sense of control and security. He also knew that hoarding tended to run in families.

There were a couple of cows grazing in the field with the junk. In a muddy area not far from the back door, three or four hogs were confined in a pen attached to the ramshackle barn.

"They're clannish," Bear was saying. "Backwoods, maybe you would call it. They raise their own food. They hunt, fish, pride themselves on living off the land. There are a lot of folks like that around here."

There as something else around here, too, Jesse thought to himself. There was a killer who was acting out his twisted fantasies.

"You ever find that missing report on Kane Blackwell?" Jesse asked.

"I sure didn't," Bear replied. "I don't know what could have happened to it."

Bear looked at Jesse. "He give you any trouble about Jenna staying with you?"

"None," Jesse replied. "You know about Jenna staying with me?"

Bear shrugged. "Hell, everyone knows everything that goes on around here. I'm glad Jenna's staying with you. With everything that's going on, I think that's just where she ought to be. This is no time for a woman to be living on her own."

As Bear pulled up to the yellow police tape and put the squad car into park, he looked into his rearview mirror. "That's not good. Take a look behind us. Looks like it's going to rain again. And hard."

He pulled the door open and went down the steps. The stairs creaked familiarly and softly beneath his weight.

In the deep silence there came the rasp of a match. He touched the flame to the wick and the lantern flared. The soft hiss of the lamp filled the room as the smell of heated kerosene permeated the damp air.

Shrouded in his raincoat, he stood looking down at her. The mattress was stained with blood all around her. Blood from the others. But her blood would soon be added, too.

Not used to the light, she averted her eyes. Well, he would damned well make sure she looked at him. He squatted down beside her and brushed the loose hair from her face. He grabbed her chin roughly. He turned her face, then snipped a lock of her hair from the back of her head and held it in his palm. The strands were dark but they had a tinge of amber in the light.

Without warning, he tore the tape from her mouth. She groaned as the pain slowly subsided.

"You're a monster," she panted.

He didn't reply. There was only the whisking sound of the wide silver tape as he pulled it off a roll, out to a length of four or five inches.

"Oh, Keara," he breathed. "You need to learn when to keep silent and to speak only when you are given permission. But," he added softly. "I'm very certain you will be a quick learner."

He pressed the new tape firmly over her mouth.

That really panicked her. She was breathing heavily through her nose. He reached out and grabbed her chin again. He turned her face this way and that. Tears had begun to form in her eyes. He smiled.

"Crying isn't going to do anything but make it harder for you to breathe."

She blinked, a new wave of terror making her go tense as she tried not to cry.

He got to his feet, still watching her. He wasn't in a hurry. A few hours like this would do wonders toward developing a stronger sense of cooperation.

He reached into his pocket, opened his hand and looked at the bracelet she had been wearing. It was a pretty bracelet that would make a nice addition to his collection. He read the inscription: *To Keara, Love Mom.*

As he read the words, a hint of bitterness curled his lips. Anger simmered just below the surface.

He got to his feet and then stared down at her. They all showed their fear eventually. There were plenty of ways to bring that out. She hadn't learned yet. First, she would have plenty of time to think about what he was going to do to her. He had certainly spent a long time thinking about it.

His gaze shifted to the mirror hanging on the wall opposite him. It was nice to see things from all perspectives. The shiny star on his chest flashed as it caught the light. Such a small thing and yet it gave him an incredible amount of authority. He had polished it up nicely. Not a finger print on it. It gleamed just like a firefly caught in a jar as he twisted his body back and forth.

His eyes went cold, however, as he remembered how the badge had been lost. For a moment his hands clenched at his sides as his thoughts focused on someone else.

Eventually she would pay, too. He needed to be patient, though. Every detail needed to be just right. Everything needed to be perfect.

He reached out and picked up the soft white cloth. He lifted the nightgown to his face and drank deeply of her perfume. He closed his eyes and the fantasy grew as he envisioned again what he would do to her and how she would plead and beg, right before he ended her life.

Chapter 20

By the end of the day, they had received a new flood of calls reporting suspicious activity. They came in the form of complaints, tips and outright accusations. The more interviews Jesse conducted, the more he learned about the hidden underbelly of Alder Grove.

The town certainly had its share of secrets. Things that were normally kept behind locked doors. But fear was making those secrets leak out like rain pouring through a sieve.

Pete Adley had been seen peeping through Betty Parn's wndow. It was the second time he had been caught doing so.

Bear responded to a call at Arlen West's house. Arlen had blown more than a dozen holes in his barn with a shot gun after a drinking spree and a fight with his wife. She was scared. It wasn't the first time a night of drinking had turned violent.

And dirt kept floating to the surface. Nelda Starling had found her husband's hidden stash of porn. Tim Ryne was having an affair with one of the tellers at the bank. Jesse also learned that Leberda Beeson smoked pot with her son, that Olin Ferrell was sending graphic pictures of his private parts to women he barely knew, and that Ebner Galt had been caught beating more than eggs in the back room of Joelle's Diner. Jesse had made a mental note not to eat there again.

It was an extension of the usual gossip, except that fear was shining a light into some of the deeper corners of the town. And a strange call had come in that afternoon. A woman who would not identify herself reported that there was something about Randal Blackwell that she thought they should know.

Unfortunately, after making the call, it seemed the woman had changed her mind. She had hung up without giving her identity or any information.

And then things hit closer to home. They learned that Dell's marriage had broken up and that his wife had filed for a divorce.

Jesse maneuvered his car around the orange cones that marked the detour he needed to take. One bridge was still closed because it had been washed out by the recent rains. He had to go about six miles out of his way, down a rough gravel road and across the creek at a point where the rock bottom was flat and smooth enough for a vehicle to pass. Then it was slow going up a steep, temporary gravel road till he made it back to the black top.

It had been a long day. He knew he needed time to think things through, but time was one thing they didn't have. He hated to think that the sun was going down and that Keara was still in the hands of a sadistic murderer.

As soon as he stepped into the house, Jesse could smell something good cooking on the stove. He went into the kitchen and lifted the top off a big pot and saw chili simmering. His stomach growled as he set his keys on the counter. He hadn't eaten since early morning.

He crossed the kitchen and looked out the screen door at the back of the house and saw Jenna and Abby in the back yard. For a while he watched without them knowing he was there.

Jenna looked as innocent and carefree as Abby as they played on the swing set. They were both wearing brightly-colored boots. Jenna had a pair that she used for gardening. Abby liked them so much that Jenna had bought Abby a pair of her own. Abby wore them everywhere.

Right now they were both swinging in the brightly-colored boots, laughing and breathless just like two little kids. Jesse hadn't seen Abby so happy since before Laney had died.

A slight frown touched his face. He had meant to talk to Jenna about that kiss in the hallway. And the other one in the hardware store.

Yeah. They needed to talk. The trouble was, there just hadn't been time. Not time alone anyway.

He hadn't had time for a lot of things. The investigations kept him tied up night and day. They hadn't been alone for two minutes. Though he conceded as how that might be a good thing.

Jenna suddenly looked up and noticed him in the doorway. Her smile grew and, against his will, something in his gut tightened as she got off the swing and came back into the house.

"How's your foot?" she asked as she stepped into the kitchen.

"Better," he lied.

"I feel guilty about you taking care of the kids all the time," he confessed. "I promised Josh two days ago that I would find the time to shoot some hoops with him."

"It's all right, Jesse. They understand. Anyway, I *shot some hoops* with him today."

"You did?"

"I did."

She walked to the stove and lifted the lid on the chili. "We waited on dinner. We thought you might be able to join us. Josh and Abby wanted chili dogs for supper. They said you liked them, too. But in case you're not in the mood for chili, I have something else." Her face brightened with a surprise. "I have absolutely everything that is needed for a killer Chicago hot dog. Even neon green relish and poppy seed buns."

"You're kidding," he said as he began to loosen his tie. He smiled in appreciation at her thoughtfulness. "Both sound good. And I'm starved. I'll probably eat both."

She picked up a spoon. Her back was to him as she stirred the chili. "I figured out your secret." She glanced at him over her shoulder. "The one you've been trying to hide."

His hand stilled on his tie. "What do you mean?"

"I mean," she said with her back still towards him. "That you add sugar when you make chili. That's the secret ingredient."

He finished undoing his tie and began to roll back his sleeves. "Well, I confess that's true. But the real secret is how *much* you add."

After dinner, alone in his room, Jesse turned to look into the mirror and frowned. There were all kinds of personality disorders. Each case was unique. Each case presented different challenges. He had to find a killer with two distinctly different faces. One was an amiable Dr. Jekyll that he presented to the world. And the other was a very evil version of Mr. Hyde who kept his identity a secret until he was ready to pounce.

She was on a staircase. Stone walls rose high above her, vanishing into darkness. Moonlight spilled through the open doorway, sifting through the tree branches outside and casting skeletal shadows on the walls.

There was a picture on the wall above her. It was a picture of one of the victims. The picture suddenly came to life. The woman in the picture was asking for help, though her words were silent.

The dream shifted and Jenna found herself in a deeper darkness, another level of the dream. She heard a voice call her name.

The voice called again and mist began to drift in eerie slow motion across the dirt floor. She realized she was in another room. A basement.

The room connected to a graveyard that continued on into the darkness. Bodies that hadn't been buried deep enough had been found because someone had forgotten to put locks on the coffins. It was sad because no one had known they were there and she could hear the voices of some of the victims calling out.

One coffin lid opened. The woman in the coffin opened her eyes and looked at Jenna. She rose up and floated out of the coffin, beckoning Jenna to follow her.

They passed a row of headstones and then another. The ghostly figure stopped, turned slowly and stared at Jenna. Her hand reached out.

The hand opened and Jenna saw that there were coins in it. Silver coins that glittered in the moonlight as they fell slowly to the ground. The hand, now empty, reached towards her, came closer and closer until it was almost touching her. Then the woman looked down, wanting Jenna to look down, too. Jenna saw that the woman wore no shoes.

Suddenly she was aware of an unpleasant odor, a mingling of old wood and mildew, of decaying leaves and the metallic smell of blood.

With a last look of sadness, the woman floated smoothly backwards until the darkness swallowed her up. Jenna wanted to leave that place too. She looked around at the basement walls and knew it was where the murders had taken place. The walls held the memories. The screams had been absorbed there, too.

Suddenly a wolf walked into the moonlight. The wolf's face transformed into the face of a man so that it was now half man, half beast. It spoke in a human voice although every now and then it would growl. And although it had been created a man, it had been trained to think that it was a wolf so that its very identity had become that of a savage beast.

It was terrifying for Jenna to realize that it also possessed the cunning, the reasoning of a man, and that it had been secretly watching her from the shadows.

While she hoped that the darkness and the mist hid her, the man-beast slowly lifted its face and looked at her, watching for a sign of weakness in her, she knew. She also knew that if she should show any fear at all, he would lunge and tear her to pieces.

The beast started moving towards her. When she tried to take a step backward, she found that she couldn't move. Her limbs were frozen, paralyzed. His teeth were razor sharp and bared. He threw his head back and howled . . .

Jenna bolted upright in bed. Her heart was pounding wildly in her chest. The terror of the dream would eventually fade, she knew. But for now she was still in the grip of fear, too afraid to move.

"Jenna."

Jesse stood in the doorway.

She didn't answer him right away.

He stepped into the room. "Are you all right? I heard you crying out in your sleep."

"Yes." She swallowed, willing her pounding heart to slow its pace. "I'm all right."

"You must have been having a nightmare. Bad?"

She nodded. The nightmare had been so vivid. It was one of those disturbing dreams that reaches deep into you though you can't explain exactly why.

Jesse stepped closer to the bed. "You sure you're all right?"

"Yes," she whispered. "It's probably because of everything that's been going on. That missing girl. Her mother's face. I can't get those things out of my mind. She's still out there and no one knows where." She shoved her loose hair out of her face. "And those pictures on the wall at the office. They're always there."

"It's enough to give anyone nightmares," Jesse said, wishing he could say something to comfort her.

149

He saw the confusion on her face, could almost feel her terror. Her hair was in disarray as it framed her face. He had the urge to take her into his arms and make her forget what had disturbed her so deeply.

"Are you going out?" she asked.

He was dressed in faded jeans and a leather jacket. In the moonlight he looked dark. Intense. And dangerous. More like some outlaw biker than a police detective. She also detected an inner tension in him, something that simmered just below the surface. She had been aware of it all evening.

"I couldn't sleep, either," he said. "I haven't had the bike out for a while. I thought I would go for a ride to clear my head."

It was true. He needed to clear his thoughts. There had been so much input these past few days that he knew he needed time alone to process it all.

The urge to hold Jenna was still there, warring with his common sense. A slight breeze came through the window. The curtains lifted. The shadows shifted across his face.

Jenna's nightgown dipped low. In the moonlight he could see the outline of her breasts. Need stirred to life deep inside him. Now wasn't the time for this, he told himself sternly. Now wasn't the time to talk to her about those kisses either. It would be a dangerous subject for him to bring up with her looking like that.

The best thing for him to do was to get out of her room before he did something stupid. Something *else* stupid.

She spoke first, making it easy for him. "All right," she said in the darkness. "I'll see you in the morning."

Chapter 21

Jesse pushed the front door of the Muddy Alley open. The bar was typically dark and the ceiling was low. The windows, bright with neon beer signs, hid the interior from the outside world. Like most bars.

Saturday night. Two more hours till closing time. He took a seat at the long bar and ordered a beer.

The place was filled with what must be the usual regulars. Some sat at the bar nursing drinks. Others sat around the tables or played pool. Everything was relatively quiet.

He had been replaying all the information he had in his mind. He was convinced that the killer was someone local. His gut also told him that someone knew something that could lead them to the killer. They just hadn't come forward yet.

He picked up his bottle and took another sip of beer. A lot of information circulated in places like this. Drinking made men, and women, more likely to talk and to share confidences.

Irita Langston, dressed differently than she dressed at the bakery, sidled up to him and took a seat to his left. She immediately struck up a conversation. He finished his beer and played a game of pool with the woman. Then they sat down to have another drink at one of the tables, because she talked almost non-stop, and because he had realized, during the conversation, that she had made the anonymous call about Randal Blackwell.

"You don't usually come in here," Irita said as she slowly twirled the plastic stick in her drink. "But I'm glad you did," she added, looking at him from beneath her dark, heavily mascaraed lashes.

"So'm I," he replied. "I needed some time to unwind."

"You're not like the usual men who hang out here," she said.

"And how's that?" he asked as he leaned back in his chair.

Randal Blackwell was also in the bar. From one of the shadowed tables along the wall, he was watching them like a hawk. Jesse noted the look in Irita's eyes as they briefly swept in the man's direction. If rumor was right, Jesse thought, the Blackwell brothers shared more than just a name.

Blackwell gave Jesse a nasty look, then hunched moodily over his drink. Other than that, he didn't cause any trouble.

"I hear that Jenna is living with you."

Jesse lifted one dark eyebrow and she explained. "Vidia Blackwell told me. Did you have a fight? Is that why you're here tonight?"

She looked hopeful, like a shark circling.

He decided it wouldn't hurt to let her believe there was trouble between Jenna and him.

"Living with Jenna can be difficult at times." That at least was the truth.

"So I've heard," Irita remarked with a toss of her chin-length, dark hair.

He took a stab. "Vidia Blackwell doesn't like Jenna very much, does she?"

The woman gave a low laugh. "Vidia doesn't like anyone, really. But you're right. She doesn't like what Jenna did to her brother, Kane."

"What exactly did she do?"

"Kicked him out."

Jesse waited and Irita added, "Jenna never fit in. She was an outsider. An import, Vidia called her."

The woman took a sip of her drink, apparently forgetting that Jesse, too, was an *import*.

"Jenna probably never had a chance of fittng in," Jesse commented quietly.

"Not a chance," Irita agreed. "Especially not with that family."

Irita ordered another drink when the waitress passed their table. Jesse sensed that she was on the verge of confiding more information, and hoped another drink might do it. He paid the waitress when she came back with the drink.

He threw out some bait. "Divorce happens all the time. Maybe she had her reasons."

"Maybe," Irita returned with a slight pout. She stared down at the drink in her hand for a moment, then almost helplessly cast a quick glance in Randal Blackwell's direction. "There are plenty of dirty little secrets around," she added enigmatically.

Jesse tried to keep the conversation going. "You can't tell what happens behind closed doors. Maybe Kane Blackwell was prone to violence."

"Did she say that?" Irita wanted to know.

"No. She doesn't talk about her marriage. But it's a common enough reason for divorce."

Irita curled her fingers tightly around her glass. "You're right. You never know what goes on behind closed doors."

Jesse suspected that he had touched on something that was making the woman uncomfortable.

"Kane had a short temper," Irita finally confided.

Jesse tried probing farther. "Who knows? Maybe he was capable of violence. Maybe not to everyone, but maybe towards women."

Direct hit. Irita had definitely reacted to that.

Randal Blackwell was watching her again, with eyes that glittered intently in the darkness. And Irita was looking back at him. Her gaze shifted back to Jesse as her lips thinned in a hard imitation of a smile.

"He seems pretty interested in what's going on over here," Jesse remarked.

"I heard about you and Rand Blackwell in the hardware store," she said. "Apparently there's more to you than meets the eye."

She gave him a not-so-subtle once over. "You're definitely different than the rest of the law around here."

She ran a finger around the rim of her glass. "Are all cops in Chicago like you?"

"I don't know about that," he answered.

She was openly, unabashedly flirting with him. He wondered if she was also trying to make Randal Blackwell jealous. Her gaze skittered over to him once again.

"Randal Blackwell doesn't look too happy about me sitting here with you."

He had no doubt that she had made that call. He wanted to know what she knew. This woman was one of the reasons Jenna had gotten a divorce, and by the looks that Randal Blackwell was giving her, she had slept with him, too. Jesse would have bet a month's pay on it.

She looked back at Jesse. "They say it's someone local, this killer. Do you think that's true?"

"He might be," Jesse replied. "How do you feel about that?"

Her gaze narrowed speculatively for a long moment. "I think people don't reveal who they really are until they get what they want from you," she said, then lifted her glass and drained it.

"There are people like that," Jesse nodded in agreement. "But not everyone's like that."

Irita, watching the waitress pass their table with a tray of food, said, "I'm hungry. The food here is good. Want to order something?"

"I've already eaten. But go ahead."

As she placed her order, he waited only half patiently, hoping that she had more to say to him. Irita was very different from Jenna, who had once confessed to him that she had been in a bar only once in her life. Irita was certainly comfortable here. He wasn't going to lecture her, but with the amount of alcohol she had consumed, he thought it was risky behavior on her part with a killer on the loose.

Unlike Irita Langston, Jenna had an innocence, a naivete, about her. Jenna wasn't like the worldly women he had met in Chicago, either. Jenna was so open and honest that it was hard for her to understand that not everyone was like she was. She believed in the innate goodness of people because she was so good herself.

His profiling had led to a sobering realization for her. In Jenna's mind, she had thought that it would be terrible for a killer to have to live with what he had done. The reality was that, for the most part, killers didn't feel remorse. They didn't feel guilt or any of the usual emotions a normal person would feel. They enjoyed killing. They looked forward to it, lived for it.

Yeah. Jenna was different than most women he had met. He liked her innocence and her openness. He liked how she completed the household and how she related to Josh and Abby.

Taking walks in the rain and catching fireflies in a jar seemed as natural to Jenna as it did to the kids. She was definitely not like any other woman he had ever met. And his feelings for her weren't like any he had ever felt before.

"You're one of the few strangers to come into this bar," Irita was saying.

He had to force himself to refocus, to concentrate on the woman before him and what she was saying.

"Maybe that's why Randal Blackwell is watching us so hard," he suggested.

She shrugged, trying to affect a nonchalance that wasn't completely convincing.

"Have you known him for a long time?" Jesse asked.

"All my life."

"You know the family well?"

"I've been best friends with Vidia Blackwell since grade school. I know them."

She shook her hair back from her face. "I do business with the family. I buy maple syrup from them in the spring. I use it in the bakery."

"That's interesting. I heard they make their own maple syrup. There was even an articlel in the paper about it."

"Yes. They do a lot of things together. They're close." She leaned forward confidentially and let her breath out in a short, cynical snort. "If people only knew how close."

She surprised him with her next statement which was delivered in a vehement tone of bitterness. "The truth is, they're terrible liars and cheats. And you had better not get on their bad side," she added darkly.

She looked like she knew something else but was trying to decide if she should share it with him. Which, of course, made Jesse want to dig deeper.

"Sounds like they're a hard bunch to do business with."

"You just have to be careful," she said.

You said you were friends with Vdia Blackwell," he probed. "Is she the same?"

"Vidia has her dark side. Kane actually is closer to my age. We were in the same grade." She frowned slightly as if recalling something unpleasant in the past. "When we were growing up, Kane always had marks and bruises on his body. He would say that he fell out of a hay mow, or tripped and hit his head on a disk, or that he fell off a tractor."

"Farming can be a dangerous occupation," Jesse commented.

"Yeah, well, farming wasn't responsible for his *accidents*." She dragged out the word. "They all got a dose of plain meanness on a daily basis. Vidia would tell me how her father actually liked killing their dogs. And once he set a cat on fire after he doused it with kerosene."

"Sounds like it was a rough place to grow up," Jesse said, watching the woman more closely.

"You don't know the half of it. They took in some cousins. Their father resented them for even being there and hated his wife for taking them in. He tolerated it. On the surface. But he was always finding ways to pit the boys against each other. He encouraged them to be as brutal as he was. The rivalry in the family was almost legendary."

"What about the mother?" Jesse asked.

"She was just as mean as he was," Irita replied with a frown. "Maybe you couldn't blame her. I mean, living with that kind of brutality day in and day out would have an effect on anyone. It must have affected them all.

"She shocked everyone one day by disappearing. She just took off and left all those kids. With *him*. She did come back after a few weeks. No one talked about it. Things went on just as if she had never left." Irita shrugged. "I remember because I would go with my mother to bring food over there when she was gone."

"Their father must have appreciated the kindness," Jesse said.

"Appreciated?" Irita echoed. "He appreciated it, all right. The ornery bastard never looked at a female without having lecherous thoughts."

Just then, Irita's food arrived and she devoted herself to her cheeseburger and fries. To be polite, Jesse paid for her food. And the drink she ordered with it.

He was amazed at how fast she packed down the cheeseburger. She offered him some of her fries and her flirting became bolder.

"You know, you don't know me very well," Jesse said to her. "For all you know, I could be this killer they're looking for."

He didn't see any fear in her eyes whatsoever at that statement. In fact, she laughed and stabbed a French fry into a pool of catsup.

"You," she said, pointing the fry at him. "Are the last person I would expect."

Chapter 22

Jesse didn't see Jenna the next morning. He got up before dawn and went to the office early. Some reports he had been waiting for were supposed to have been faxed in. They weren't there.

He kept replaying what Irita Langston had told him last night. Certainly the Blackwell family could be called severely dysfunctional, but they weren't the only ones like that around. He wanted that report on Kane Blackwell but it was still missing and no copies could be found anywhere.

Bear had left him a list of the people who had volunteered to search for the missing girl. Serial killers tended to have a fascination with law enforcement. Especially when it came to the crimes they themselves had committed. Being a part of the investigation gave them a warped sense of power and control.

Jesse looked over the list of searchers. No Blackwells there.

He had just set the list back on his desk when a call came in. One of the search dogs had found something.

While Gussie put the finishing touches on a casserole, Jenna made herself a cup of tea and sat down at the table.

"t's a shame you having to work on a weekend," Gussie said over her shoulder.

"I only have to go in for about an hour or so and take care of some things I didn't get to yesterday. There's so much going on down there. Everyone is putting in long hours."

"I imagine they are," Gussie said as she dried her hands on a dish towel. "Jesse works day and night these days. You should both take some time off. Together."

Jenna looked up from her cup of tea. She had not failed to notice the change in the woman's tone. "What do you mean?" she asked.

Gussie didn't answer right away. She carefully folded the towel and hung it back on the towel rack. Oh, mercy," she said as she suddenly turned. "Every time you two are in the same room together, it's as plain as day."

Jenna stared at the woman. Was her attraction to Jesse that obvious?"

She didn't know what to say. "What's as plain as day?"

"Not that it's any of my business," Gussie went on. "But I'm not the only one around here that would be tickled if you two got together."

"Gussie," Jenna began. "I have gotten over one divorce. A relationship now, this soon- Well, I don't know how I would handle that."

"Soon?" Gussie echoed. "Jenna, you have been divorced for over two years now. And besides, Jesse is not Kane. If you ask my opinion, you were lucky to get out of that marriage."

Gussie brought her own cup of tea to the table and sat down across from Jenna.

"Your divorce didn't surprise me in the least," she said. "Kane was always selfish and mean-spirited. He got that from his father. Oh, he knew how to pretend to be something different, all right. But deep down, he was another person. Sneaky is what he was. I figured that out a long time ago."

"Did you know the family well?" Jenna asked. There had always been questions about Kane's past, things that he had refused to talk about.

Gussie took a sip of her tea and set her cup back down, narrowing her eyes as if she was looking into the distant past. "Well enough," Gussie replied. "Rogan Blackwell did his best to destroy that family. He was a black-hearted man who wanted his family to pay for all the misery he had ever had in his own life. Those kids knew nothing but anger and violence from the moment they were born."

Gussie took another sip of her tea, looking as if she had just washed down something bitter. "You can't expect to raise children on that and not leave a mark on them."

"Why was he like that?" Jenna asked. "It must have started somewhere."

"Why? Who knows. Rogan Blackwell didn't need a reason to be mean, it seemed. All I know is that he wasn't happy unless those kids were at each other's throats. He enjoyed it. It was like a game with him."

"What was Kane's mother like? He said he was close to her."

Gussie pursed her lips tightly together for a moment. "Nothing could be further from the truth. Vetta wasn't close to any of her children. But she seemed to hold a special animosity towards Kane.

"She was once a steady church goer," Gussie went on. "We went to the same church. But then something happened. Maybe it was all the contention of those years that wore her down." Gussie shook her head slowly. "One day she just up and left. Left all the kids behind. Of course, everyone was shocked by it. The ladies down at the church decided to help out. We took turns checking on the kids. Made sure they went to school and got fed.

"Well, Vetta did finally come back home. One day I took a casserole over to the house. She could barely drag herself out of bed. She kept talking, but she wasn't making much sense. She went on about her sister being pregnant at the same time, as if that was a scandal. She cried about things like wickedness and sin. I couldn't understand it and I was worried about her. I thought she was going through some kind of a breakdown, the poor soul."

"So what happened to her?"

"Eventually she snapped out of whatever it was. Some people whispered it was because of the change. But that couldn't have been true because it turned out she was pregnant. Maybe it did have something to do with hormones.

"The story whispered around," Gussie continued. "Was that Rogan accused her of running off with another man, but there was never any proof that that's what happened. And she did come back to him. Anyway, she was never the same after that. It seemed like she became as mean as he was. Then," Gussie gave her a significant look. "There was the murder. That was another terrible blow for her."

"It would be terrible for any mother to lose a child," Jenna murmured sympathetically.

Gussie pressed her lips together. "They said robbery was the motive for the murder, that some antique coins had been stolen. But to my way of thinking, there was more to it. I believe it started long ago, at the beginning."

"What do you mean?" Jenna asked. "What started?"

"Vetta wasn't from around here. She had left her family to come here and marry Rogan Blackwell. I heard it said that she'd had a hard life before she even met Rogue. That's what they called him. If you knew the man, you would realize it was a fitting name. Anyway, the rumors were that both Vetta's parents had been heavy drinkers and that she hadn't had much of a childhood.

"After she moved here, Rogue never missed an opportunity to make her feel like she had come from trash. He called her family misfits and worthless drunks. I guess that was his way of beating her down emotionally to a place where she was lower than him."

Gussie sighed over her cup of tea. "If he had put half as much love into his marriage as he put hate, he would have had something. But he didn't. He even got at her through the kids. He ruined them, made them like he was. And I swear it was just done to spite her. Seems like he wanted her to be completely isolated and alone. It was like he wanted to punish her.

"Well, the death of her son just about put Vetta in the grave, too. I saw her twice after that. Once right before she died."

"How did she die?" Jenna wanted to know.

"It was a sudden thing," Gussie replied. "Heart failure, they said. But- "

Jenna waited for her to go on.

"Afterward, Rogue Blackwell didn't act like a man who had just lost his wife. And- "

"And?" Jenna prompted.

"He wanted her buried quick and simple. And that's the way it was. As quick and simple as it gets. But I saw him smile, Jenna. The day of the funeral, when he thought no one was looking, he sat back as if he didn't have a care in the world, and smiled. And I heard him say with my own ears, 'I can finally have some peace now.'"

"You don't think it's possible that- " Jenna's voice faded before she finished. She couldn't even say the words. It was too terrible.

"I couldn't help but wonder," Gussie answered the unasked question. "And after what I have told you, you're even wondering." She shrugged. "Everyone said she died of a broken heart. Who would question that after what she had been through? Sad, though, how life went on just the same without her. It seemed she was just forgotten."

"By her children, too?" Jenna asked.

Gussie lifted her shoulders in a shrug again. "They barely spoke of her. At least Vidia and Kane never did. Who knows what went through their minds? Maybe they thought it was weak to show their grief. Rogue ruled his family with an iron hand. He kept them close. Maybe too close. Kane especially was close to his father. He didn't seem to have his own identity. It was like he was smothered under his father's stronger personality. Funny how Kane idolized a father who put so much effort into terrorizing him."

"How did he do that? Terrorize him?" Jenna asked, not sure she wanted to hear the answers.

"Well, for one thing, have you ever wondered why Kane is so afraid of snakes? His father would scare him with them all the time. I saw him lock Kane in a tractor cab once that had a snake in it. I will never forget the look on that boy's face."

Gussie got up from the table and took her tea cup to the sink. "Rogue and Vetta are both dead now. The past is the past. It won't do anyone any good to dig up any rotten bones."

"Whose birthdays are these?"

Jenna and Gussie both turned and stared at Abby who had just come into the kitchen. "What, Abby?" Jenna asked.

"Are these somebody's birthdays?" Abby had picked up several sheets of paper from the counter.

"Oh, no, Abby. Those are some papers from work."

She didn't explain that those were the dates, or the approximate dates, of the murders. She took the papers from Abby.

"They do look like they could be birthdays, though, couldn't they?" Jenna said as she folded the papers and put them in her purse.

"Gussie?" she said. "Before I go to the office, I'm going to run out to my house and pick up some things. I need some more clothes."

"Ae you sure you should go alone?" Gussie asked.

"I'll be fine," Jenna assured her. "It's daylight and I'm not going to stay long. I'll take Max with me. He likes car rides."

Max, hearing his name, suddenly got to his feet. He looked expectantly at Jenna with his tail wagging hopefully.

Jenna opened the screen door and Max raced straight for the car. Five minutes later he was hanging his head out the window, happily biting at the rush of wind against his face. He was still enjoying the wind when Jenna turned down the gravel road that led to her house.

The sun had vanished behind a bank of storm clouds. Without the sun's warmth, the temperature dropped quickly. Good thing she was getting some clothes, Jenna thought as she slid the key into the lock. She would grab a few sweaters, too.

During her ride, she had thought about what Gussie had said about her and Jesse. She thought about it a lot. All the way over here, in fact. Something was happening to her and she didn't know if she could stop it. She didn't know if she wanted to stop it. She sighed later as she stood in her living room and looked around. She had gotten so used to living with Jesse and the kids that this place seemed empty now, as if something was missing.

Her conversation with Gussie also had her thinking about Kane's past. She went to the closet and pulled out the heavy box that belonged to Kane and slid it over to the sofa. Jesse had mistakenly brought it with her other boxes.

She sat down, picked up the album on top and set it on her lap. She reached down to another album underneath. A third album joined the others on her lap. She brushed off the dust and opened the book to the pictures that had not been looked at for many years. Pictures that maybe nobody wanted to look at.

She found the picture of the father and the children. Rogan Blackwell was standing behind Kane. His heavy jaw was raised, as if he was challenging the person taking the picture.

Jenna finished looking through the album and then went through the other ones. And then it suddenly struck her. There were no pictures of Kane's mother. She had not seen a single one.

There had to be a picture of the woman somewhere. She dug out the last album at the bottom of the box, one she had never looked at before. Finally, her search led her to a picture of Vetta Blackwell.

She had been a small woman. She must have been pretty once, but the photo reflected a tired, hopeless look in eyes that told a great deal, especially now that Jenna knew her story. Her smile seemed forced. She did not look happy to Jenna, but perhaps she was reading too much into the picture. It was only a moment captured from a lifetime of moments.

Scarred by a difficult childhood, had she married Rogan Blackwell because she thought she could escape from that hard life, or did she subconsciously seek its continuation? What secrets were concealed behind those eyes? What lay hidden behind that sad smile?

As Jenna searched through more photographs, she lost track of time. Only Max's muffled barking from the car made her look up and realize that she had been looking at the albums for nearly an hour.

She was about to put the albums back in the box when she discovered that, in one of the picture frames, there was a picture behind another one. One corner of the top picture was folded back so that a small portion of the picture underneath could be seen. Jenna opened the back of the frame, slid the top picture out and looked at the photograph underneath.

There was a group of children, but they were older in this picture. Jenna removed the photo and held it up to the light. It was damaged by scratch marks. She looked at it closer. There were the cousins, she realized. Their names were written at the bottom.

One of them was Slater Young, the cousin who was in jail for the murder of Nolan Blackwell. He looked like the Blackwell brothers. A little in the eyes. And the hair was the same color. He definitely had the same jaw line, only it was a little more pronounced.

Jenna blinked and looked at the picture closer. How could they have the same jaw line when it had been passed down through the father? It wasn't possible, unless-

Unless Rogan Blackwell was the father of this boy, too. That would make them brothers, not cousins. That meant that-

The shocking truth hit her like an unexpected blow. That meant that Rogan Blackwell had gotten his wife's sister pregnant. It was the only explanation.

Had they known? Someone, somewhere along the line, must have seen the resemblance and put things together. Jenna thought back through all that Gussie Hester had told her. Vetta Blackwell had talked about her sister being pregnant at the same time. And about sin. And wickedness. Did she mean adultery? The pieces seemed to fit. If anything could cause a breakdown, wouldn't that?

If Vetta Blackwell had taken her sister's children into her home, they would have been a constant reminder of her husband's infidelity. She must have been aware of the resemblance. She must have worried that someone else would eventually figure it out, too. Gussie said Rogan Blackwell had turned the children into what he was. What exactly did that mean?

A thousand questions were turning over in her mind. She dug deeper into the box. There were some loose papers at the bottom. She didn't know if they were more pictures or something else.

There were several envelopes. One of the envelopes was very heavy. Jenna opened it and discovered that it contained a gray cloth sack. She unfolded the worn sack, which was tightly bound with a leather cord. She removed the cord and part of the contents fell into her lap. The rest of the contents scattered across the living room floor.

Jenna stared at the silver coins. There were dozens of them. Antique coins. A cold chill ran through her blood.

She found a single, yellowed envelope. It contained school reports. There was also a list of dates. As she read over what was written on the paper, she drew in a sudden shocked gasp. The hand holding the paper began to shake.

Abby had been right. The missing connection was birthdays. The birthdays listed for the children were almost identical to the dates of the murders.

She straightened, startled, because over Max's barking she heard another noise. She started to rise up from the sofa. Several coins slid down between the cushions. She ignored them. She realized she had not locked the doors, but she hadn't anticipated staying so long.

The sound she heard, she realized, was the back door slowly creaking open. She held her breath and stared at the man who suddenly appeared in the doorway.

"Surprised to see me?" Kane asked as a slow smile curled the corners of his mouth.

Chapter 23

Jesse slowed down as he approached the same detour location he had passed for the past few days. The orange and black detour sign was still up ahead and traffic had come to a standstill, making him wonder what was holding things up.

He picked up his cell phone from the seat beside him and punched in a number. He got the same recorded message he had listened to ten minutes ago. He left a brief message for a call back and sighed in frustration. "Where are you, Jenna?" he asked out loud.

He flipped the phone close. Traffic started moving again and he turned off the blacktop onto the temporary gravel road.

It was late when he arrived back at the office. Two members of the task team were still there.

"We're going out for pizza," one of them told him. "Want to come with us?"

"Thanks, but I still have some work to do."

After the door closed behind the two men, Jesse picked up his cell phone and tried Jenna again. "Come on, Jenna, answer your phone."

She didn't answer and he didn't see any sense in leaving another message. He got up and went into the other room. He stood looking up at the photographs of the victims.

They had missed something. But what? he wondered in frustration. What they needed were answers, not more questions.

He thought about his talk with Irita Langston. Randal Blackwell had a history of questionable behavior, though there was nothing concrete to bring him in for questioning on.

Keara Eland didn't fit the pattern of the other women. Jesse knew that the killer was methodical. Organized. Precise. Everything was planned down to the smallest details. But something had changed. Something had made him go after two girls instead of one. And Keara had dark hair, unlike the others.

What compulsion was driving the killer? He kept his victims for days. But why Keara? Jesse ran his hand over the harsh growth of whiskers on his face, felt the pressure of time running out . . .

He stopped, his hand stilling on his jaw.

Running out of time.

Time. Was it the key element here? The more he thought about it, the more his gut told him that it made sense. If the dates were important, how did he tie them together?

He checked his inbox and realized that today's mail had not yet been distributed. Which meant that Jenna had not come to the office to take care of it as she had planned. Maybe Josh or Abby needed her for something. Jenna often changed her plans to accommodate their schedules.

He looked on her desk. The mail was still there. He picked up a small package addressed to him. It contained his new badge. He shuffled some loose mail and found the report he had been waiting for.

He looked over more details about the mortar mixture from the other bodies. The gravel on both bodies was nearly identical in composition to the gravel from the body washed up in the creek. That was not a surprise to him.

He also found the fax he had been waiting for and a hand-written note from a friend in the Chicago crime lab. He quickly scanned the note. It read:

Hey, Jesse. We have been working day and night on this to try and get you some answers. A lot of evidence was undoubtedly washed away by the flood waters. We did find a plant seed specimen on the clothing from the barbed wire. I sent it to another lab, to an expert in forensic botany and you should have the report in a few days. You will get the exact technical classification soon, but here's what got my attention. The same seeds were found on the clothing of Jana Calder. Thought you would find that interesting.

The seeds are commonly called sticktights. They're fairly wide spread in the state, and these might have been picked up at any point, but we both know that sometimes something small can end up being important. The little hitchhikers will hold fast to anything. At some point the victims were in an overgrown or untended area of high weeds.

But the really interesting thing that we found was maple syrup. Not just any kind of maple syrup. The pure, raw stuff, with enough impurities and foreign matters, ashes and trace amounts of insects and plant debris, to say with a certainty that the stuff was homemade. Straight from the trees.

Jesse was about to reach for his phone again when he saw another envelope addressed to him. There was no return address in the upper left hand corner. He tore the envelope open.

A chill ran straight up his spine as he read the hand-written sheet of paper and realized it had become personal.

I'm sitting here watching the moonlight on the water. I see a reflection of the stars. A star. One that has fallen into my grasp. Twinkle, twinkle little star. Up above the world so high.

Hell, everyone looks up to a star. You should be more careful. Your losses could become very costly. You know as well as I do that you can't stop the darkness from falling. And in that darkness, I'll bet you can't make a woman scream the way I can.

There was no doubt in Jesse's mind that the note was from the killer. What had fallen into his grasp? Another victim? Keara Eland? Or a badge. His badge. Maybe both.

He was on the phone again. He called for a police car to go out to his house. He interpreted he note as a warning. Then he made a call to his house.

"You mean she never showed up at work?" On the other end of the phone, there was worry in Gussie Hester's voice. "I told her she shouldn't go back there alone."

"Go where?"

"To her house. I stayed here because she said she would be back in a couple of hours. But that was more than three hours ago. Jenna is usually so prompt."

Fear stabbed a path straight through Jesse's chest. Before he had even hung up with Gussie, he was on his way out the door.

"You were going through my things. What were you looking for?"

Jenna was still trying to process all that she had found in the box. Kane must have known about the coins hidden in the bottom of box. He didn't seem surprised to see the coins scattered across the floor. He must have also known that the murder thirteen years ago had not been committed by his cousin. The coins were proof of that. Had Kane committed the murder? Had he killed his own brother?

"I asked you a question."

Jenna knew she had to think her way carefully through this. She glanced at the door. She wished she had brought Max in the house with her.

"It's Rand," she heard Kane say. "Rand is the one who has been killing those women."

His statement shocked her. But the bland tone of Kane's voice and the vacant stare in his eyes made her wonder if he was telling her the truth. She wouldn't expect Kane to simply throw his brother to the wolves like that.

She had to leave, before he had too much time to think about all this. Before he figured out that she knew too much.

But before she could reach the door, he grabbed her arm and stopped her. She fought his hold on her, but he yanked her arm hard and spun her around, slamming her up against the wall. Before she knew what was happening, he had snapped a pair of handcuffs on her. It was so quick and so unexpected that they were locked in place before she even knew what was happening.

"What are you doing?"

"We're going for a ride," he told her.

"Going where?"

"You'll see when we get there."

Jenna could read nothing in his eyes. They were cold and completely emotionless. And it was that very coldness that frightened her more than anything else.

Kane wouldn't answer her questions. He wouldn't even look at her. He continued to stare straight ahead as he drove. The confining position of her arms and the handcuffs cut off the circulation in her hands. Focus, she told herself. Panic wasn't going to help. But panic kept mounting in spite of her efforts to control it.

She didn't know where they were going. She didn't know if this was some kind of plan to protect his brother. Or the Blackwell name.

"Kane, please. These are hurting my arms."

He continued to ignore her. He turned off the blacktop and the car bumped roughly along the gravel road in front of his sister Vidia's house.

Another woman looked into an oval mirror hanging on the wall before her. The glass gave back a distorted image, full of ripples and imperfections. The mirror had been old even when she was a little girl.

Darkness had fallen and the night was filled with the chirping of frogs and crickets. But aside from those sounds, the night was as deep and silent as a grave.

She lifted the tube of lipstick to her mouth. Slowly and carefully she traced her pale, thin lips. The candlelight brought out beautifully the contrasting color of the dark lipstick against her lighter skin. And the silver in her hair almost looked like gold. You couldn't see the fine lines that etched the places where unhappiness had settled.

Anyone seeing her with even a stitch of makeup on would have been surprised. Shocked even. She didn't go about in broad daylight like this. She wouldn't dare. But at night when she was alone, she was drawn, almost irresistibly.

She had seen the car pass by slowly. She had watched as the headlights probed the overgrown field to the west. She had even lingered at the window as the car turned onto the gravel road.

They were pretty. Every one of them. She looked back into the murky depths of the mirror. Somehow it made it all seem normal in some unfathomable way.

"Painted up in falseness," came a harsh echo from the past. "Vanity has a price, Vidia."

She knew it was true. Her mother had told her it was so many times. Just as her mother had told her, after catching her playing with her makeup, that she could put on all the paint that she wanted, but she would never, ever be pretty. And deep down, Vidia believed, straight down to her broken heart, that it was true. She would never be more than she was.

Chapter 24

Kane turned off the engine and the lights and pocketed the keys. He seemed to be lost in thought as he stared at the dark woods that surrounded the truck. Finally he said, "You've already figured something out. Or you think you have. Don't lie and try to deny it."

"I *am* wondering," she said. "Why you are doing this."

"So we can be alone," he answered her. "And you are obviously curious about this place."

The old Blackwell house looming up before them looked even more sinister by moonlight. Kane shifted in his seat and turned his body toward her. "Relax. Everything is going to work out."

He continued to watch her face closely. "We both know you're smart enough to have figured some things out. You found the coins. They're hard evidence, I suppose."

She didn't want to ask the question, but there was no way around it. "Is it true what you said about Rand?"

"Rand? No, I was only kidding."

No one would joke about that. And he hadn't looked like he was kidding. He had looked deadly serious.

"Are you going to take these handcuffs off me?"

"I can't do that."

He straightened his body out and rested his head against the back of the seat. He was silent as he stared up at the moon. "Thirteen years," he said almost wearily and shook his head before he turned his face to look at her again. "It's a long time."

She waited for him to go on. She had no choice there.

"If it had gotten around that we were brothers, not cousins . . . " His voice trailed off. He gave her a faint, wolfish smile. "You don't look surprised. So you *had* figured it out."

He didn't give her a chance to reply. He frowned and said, "And then when Nolan found out, well, things got out of hand. Rand tried to reason with him. But Nolan couldn't let it go." He shook his head again. "What could Rand do? Was he supposed to sit back and let us all be destroyed?"

She dreaded the answer, but she had to ask, "Is that why Slater Young vowed vengeance on everyone? Because he went to prison for a murder he didn't commit?"

"Oh, he was guilty enough," Kane replied bitterly. "He was the reason for all the trouble. He always was. You can't imagine what the bastard was capable of. Yeah, we set him up. It was the only way. It was payback for all the hell he put us through all those years. But you know what they say. Paybacks can be hell." His grin was macabre in the wan moonlight.

"What Rand did, he did for all of us," he went on.

It was hard for her to take it all in. Randall Blackwell had killed his own brother. And Kane had known all along.

"When Nolan threatened to tell," Kane said. "Rand stopped him the only way he could. He didn't want to do it. It just happened. When we found out, we decided on a plan that would keep Rand from going to jail. And tie up all the loose ends *and* get that bastard Slater out of our lives for good. Or at least for a good long time. And if it wasn't for you sticking your nose where it didn't belong, no one would have ever known."

He looked up at the house. There were no lights anywhere. Lost in thought, Kane tapped the edge of a long, lethal-looking knife on the steering wheel.

"You don't understand loyalty," he said. "I see it differently than you do. I spent my entire life learning about loyalty. And survival."

Kane gave her a long, thoughtful look. "Pretty much like you spent our entire marriage trying to prove you could survive on your own. Without any help from me." And then he seemed to be talking to himself. "Women always think they're so independent. Until you show them how vulnerable they can be." He shook his head as if trying to clear it.

"I sometimes wonder how different things would have been if they hadn't come along. Our *special* cousins, I mean." He cleared his throat

171

and went on. "They would disappear only to show up again months later. Do you know how we felt when we would see that blue car pulling into the driveway and them getting out with their stupid little red and blue suitcases? Circus suitcases. That's what Rand called them.

"They always got treated better than we did," he said with bitter mockery edging into his voice. "They couldn't do anything wrong. We always took the blame for them. It didn't take them long to learn that they could get away with murder. Slater was the worst. He didn't leave any of us alone. He tortured all of us in one way or another. He was one cold-hearted bastard. If we had a pet, it ended up dead. Every time.

"You get used to it. Death. You learn to deal with it. And about the only thing that makes you feel good about it is to accept it. To expect it. After six dead pets, you start to see things differently.

"Yeah, they were special all right. I still remember my tenth birthday. 'Can't have it this year, Kane. Not enough money.' Had one for that worthless sonofabitch though."

"And Slater," she asked. "Did he know the truth?"

"That's the million dollar question," Kane replied. "Maybe he thinks he'll have the last laugh. Not that we would allow it, of course."

"Does Vidia know?"

"Vidia," Kane sighed the name. "Slater made life a living hell for her. He was- quite insatiable in his demands. She couldn't go to anyone else for help, so she came to me. By then I was big enough to make a difference. I took care of things for her. And she was grateful."

At the word grateful, a sickness welled up in the pit of Jenna's stomach. Her thoughts must have shown in her eyes.

"She was willing," Kane told her. "It shows you how fear will make a person do anything." He narrowed his eyes as if seeing into the past. "When I beat Slater up, they punished me. They should have thanked me. But I learned a long time ago that life isn't fair. Especially for Vidia. Dear old Mom could be heartless all right. But she saved it all for us. Vidia never told. And I never did, of course. Our mother would have found a way to blame her. And aside from making life miserable for Vidia, she would have told everyone. How do you think Nolan found out about Slater? She told him. So, as always, she was behind it all.

"When she caught me and Vidia together one night, she beat the tar out of me. And then because that wasn't enough, she locked me in the barn for the rest of the day and that entire night. Said she couldn't stand the sight of me. She knew damned well the place was crawling with snakes." Hi mouth thinned and grew taut. "I think she almost smiled when she closed that door."

Clouds drifted across the face of the moon. The shadows from the barn bled into the shadows of the trees.

"I once saw a blacksnake in the rafters that had to be seven feet long. Get locked in the dark with something like that and I can assure you, you come out a changed person."

The moonlight gleamed in his eyes as the moonlight came out again. "Viddy got beat, too, almost but not quite as bad. Of course, she didn't touch her precious Slater. I wonder what Mom would have thought if she knew that one of her special adopted kids was forcing her daughter to do all kinds of nasty things. That's what she allowed into our house. She always felt sorry for them. She should have saved some of that pity for her own kids."

Kane leaned back in his seat. "The old bitch is dead and buried in the cemetery, but I can almost hear her sometimes." He was looking up at the house, a haunted expression on his face. "She never stops," he said in a voice barely above a whisper. "The doctor thought it was her heart." The mockery was back, with a hard edge to it. "But it couldn't have been her heart. She didn't have one. So Dad took care of things."

The revelation shocked her. Kane knew that his father had killed his mother. Maybe they all knew.

"It took her a long time to die. I guess some people are too mean to die easy."

"It must have been hard for your mother to have known that your father- " Jenna began but Kane cut her off.

"Slept with that whoring mother of theirs?" he finished. "She knew all right. But she still welcomed the bastard offspring into our house. Sometimes I wonder if she didn't do it to punish Dad. She was like that. Bitter. Vindictive. Maybe it was her way of constantly throwing it in his face." He frowned and shrugged off the recollection.

"Don't look so horrified. Or so innocent. That's not going to work anymore. You're living with one of your co-workers. In sin. Rand told me how you couldn't keep your hands off each other in the hardware store. You think I can't figure out what goes on when you're alone with him behind closed doors?"

He leaned towards her. "You're alone with me now. And you're afraid." His tone was low and exultant. "Don't try to deny it. When you lied about there not being anything between you and him, I knew you were no different than the rest of them. You fooled me for a while, but that won't happen again. I thought there might have been a chance for us," He turned his face. "But you made your choice already, Jenna."

He looked at her with cold, unblinking eyes. "You have only yourself to blame, you know. Like I said, paybacks are hell."

"I'll be honest with you." His fingers lightly brushed her hair. "I have been waiting for this for a very long time." His voice changed. He ran the back of his hand slowly down the side of her face. "I have dreamt about you this way. Helpless. Staring at me just the way you are now. You look so beautiful in the moonlight. Amazing how fear can transform a person."

He stopped, laughed under his breath and got out of the car. He walked around to the passenger door and pulled it open. "Let's take a moonlight walk," he said, dragging her from the car when she resisted. "Remember? We did that on our first date." He jerked her forward. "But we'll have more time for reminiscing later."

Except for a few random shafts of moonlight piercing the tightly-curtained windows, the house was dark as they went inside. Kane led her to the basement stairs. Jenna stared down into an inky blackness that terrified her.

Kane switched on a flashlight and a beam of light probed the darkness below. As Kane forced her down the steep wooden stairs, she stumbled down the last two steps. She almost fell to her knees on the concrete floor at the bottom.

"See?" she heard Kane say in the dim light. "If I wasn't here to help you, you could have gotten badly hurt."

The cold dampness closed in around her, filling her lungs with stale, musty air. The narrow beam of the flashlight moved around the space, sweeping the low ceiling and the dark walls of mortared stone.

Kane let go of her for a moment. She heard the rasp of a match and he lit a kerosene lamp. She saw someone lying on a mattress on the floor. A woman was lying with her face away from them. Like Jenna, her arms were tied behind her. Her legs were bound with duct tape. There was no way for Jenna to know if she was alive or dead. Was it Keara Eland? she wondered.

Some wooden crates were stacked against one wall. Rows of shelves were lined with dusty jars that gleamed darkly among the cobwebs. A heavy work table took up another wall. A roll of duct tape and a coiled rope were among the items on the tabletop.

Jenna was quickly going over everything Jesse had taught her about self-defense. Don't stay to fight it out with an attacker, he had told her. Get away as fast as you can. But there was nowhere to go. She couldn't outrun Kane, not with her hands tied. She shouldn't have let him get her this far. She should have fought him at the beginning.

Kane's back was to her. He was leaning over something on the table. Desperation drove her to try and escape. She made it up two steps. Three . . .

She cried out as her head jerked back. Kane had gripped her hair in his fist. A sharp agony shot through her neck as it was wrenched back.

Furious over her attempt to escape him, Kane dragged her back down the stairs. He spat out a vile profanity and swung his open hand. The blow drove Jenna to her knees. She swayed, dazed, her face stinging hotly from the blow.

"Get up," Kane hissed.

The shifting of her weight on her knees on the gravel floor was an agony. She tasted blood in her mouth.

Kane pulled her roughly to her feet. When she had managed to stand on her own, another backhanded blow slammed her into the wooden table. She felt the hard edge cut into her lower back.

As Kane loomed over her, Jenna could detect no remorse over what he had just done. His face was a mask of cold rage.

"Pay attention, Jenna," he gritted between clenched teeth. "And listen good. I own you. I owned you the moment you promised to honor and obey me. Till death do us part. Remember?"

He pulled her hard against his body. Grabbing another fistful of her hair, he pressed a knife against her arched throat. "You'll learn, Jenna, to do everything I tell you. You'll do it willingly."

He shoved her down to the mattress. "And in the end," he promised evilly. "You will beg for the chance to please me. That respect you couldn't give me before?" he said as he held her down. "You were right when you said you earn it, and I'm going to spend the next few days doing my best to earn it, every bit of it."

The duct tape hissed as he unrolled it and wound it around her ankles. Too tight, the tape dug into her skin. Realizing her helplessness, Jenna felt a new wave of terror wash over her.

175

Kane reveled at the thought of his power over her. He watched her fear, which only added to his excitement. He longed to hurt her, to bring her even further down.

"You didn't know that I watched you when you slept." He laughed at the startled look in her eyes. "But that's what you get for deciding to live alone. A woman alone is always vulnerable."

He removed one of her shoes. She couldn't suppress a shudder of revulsion as he caressed the bare foot. He removed the other shoe, running his hand slowly over that foot.

"Your boyfriend isn't the only one who can read clues." He chuckled. "Or plant them. I thought that might interest you."

He watched her closely, as a cat might watch a mouse. There was something sly in his eyes now, and in the slow, careful way he spoke. "Trace, it's called," he went on. "Hair and fibers on the body. That black hair of his, they say he's part Indian, I hear. Got some savage blood in is veins."

Jenna had learned over the years that ignorance and prejudice ran strong n the Blackwell family. She had always hated it.

"I have never scalped anyone before," Kane purred. "Now that might be interesting."

Knowing the gruesome details of the murders, Jenna knew that Kane was capable of anything.

"Your detective boyfriend is about to find himself involved in a deeper game," he said as he leaned over her. "One that he will lose and I will win. When I heard that you had let him kiss you, I knew that I would have to teach you both a lesson. And that girl- What's her name? Abby. That's right."

Not Abby, Jenna thought with panic. She couldn't bear the thought of Abby in the hands of this monster. Never in her life had she wanted to destroy someone. She wanted to destroy Kane now.

"When things start hitting a little closer to home, people will start taking a closer look."

Kane taped her mouth. He cut the tape with his knife and sat back on his heels.

"We don't have another vacancy in my little hotel yet." His eyes moved across the bed to the other woman. "But we will soon."

He passed a loop of rope around Jenna's throat and then secured the other end to one of the legs of the heavy table.

"That should hold you till I get back. Don't worry about getting lonely," he said as he got to his feet. "I won't be gone long."

He extinguished the lamp and the basement was thrown into complete blackness. Jenna listened to Kane's footsteps on the gravel floor. She heard him climb the wooden steps, heard the door at the top of the stairs creak on its hinges. The wooden latch scraped as it a lifted and then slid back into place.

She traced Kane's steps above her as he crossed the kitchen. There was another slight creak as the kitchen door opened and closed again. She heard Kane's car start up and drive away.

Jenna knew very well why she had been brought here. To become another victim. She didn't waste any time. She had to find a way to escape. Now. Not only did her life depend upon it, but the other woman's did as well. Jenna knew she was alive. She had heard her moan in the darkness.

Jenna was shaking from the adrenaline surging through her veins. The basement was cold, but sweat beaded along her brow.

There was not even a glimmer of light anywhere around her, but earlier she had seen a glint of light on a shard of glass on the concrete floor. Somewhere in the inky blackness was a piece of glass, and it wasn't far away from her. She slid over to the edge of the mattress. Her legs rolled off the mattress onto the cold, rough floor. The rope around her neck tightened. Her neck arched as she moved over the floor to where she thought the glass must be.

She reached the limit of the rope and had to twist her body over the floor. She groaned as the gravel dug painfully into her flesh. But she kept going. She knew that unless she got away now, she was never going to escape. And Abby-

She forced those thoughts out of her mind and found a new determination. She wasn't going to give up without a fight.

Every second mattered, she knew. But finding the glass seemed to take forever. The tape was cutting off the circulation in her arms. With maddening slowness, she worked her bound hands over the ground inch by painful inch. She strained her body, sliding it one way and then another. The pan in her shoulders was intense. The rope around her neck was getting tighter. She imagined there were probably hundreds of disgusting spiders and bugs crawling all over the floor, but bugs and spiders were the least of her worries right now.

She heard the woman beside her moan again as she passed the side of her hand over the ground once more. She drew it back sharply as glass cut her finger.

It was a slow and painstaking process but she finally picked the glass up between her fingers. It was even harder to work the glass back and forth across the duct tape. It was all she could do to hold it in the right position. She dropped it once and knew she couldn't afford to do that again. Finding and picking the glass up again lost precious time.

She felt the slick wetness of blood on her hands but she kept going. Concentrate, she told herself. Don't think about the blood. Ignore the pain. Ignore the strain in her muscles.

How long, she wondered, had the other woman been tied up? If she felt so uncomfortable already, how bad was it for her? And what had Kane done to her already?

Finally Jenna felt the tape slacken. And then it separated as the last inch of connecting tape was severed.

Jenna tore her hands apart then soon had the tape around her mouth pulled off. She drew in deep breaths of air. She removed the tape around her ankles next. Then the rope around her neck was thrown off.

Her heart was pounding heavily in her chest. Her breath was coming in quick gasps. She had to feel her way over to the other woman. She ran her hands over the tape and the ropes that bound her. In the darkness, removing them seemed to take an eternity. Finally both women were free.

"Are you Keara Eland?" Jenna asked.

She heard a sob in the darkness and a tearful, whispered, "Yes."

Disoriented in the darkness, both women stood up. Keara almost collapsed against Jenna.

"I'm sorry. I'm so weak," Keara said. "I haven't had any food or water- "

"Lean on me," Jenna said. "We're going to get out of here," she said with determination, as much to convince herself as Keara.

First they had to find the stairway that led out of the basement. Holding onto Keara, Jenna groped her way through the darkness. The gravel was rough and cold under her bare feet, but they were soon gripping the handrail and they began to climb the steps.

While Jenna held onto the rail, Keara held onto her as if she were a lifeline. They reached the top of the stairs and then stopped by the wooden door. Jenna paused, leaning against the rough boards.

With every nerve strained, she listened for any sound on the other side of the door. She was able to open the old latch only because she had seen how it worked when she was in the house with Jesse.

She eased the door open, wincing at the slow creak which sounded as loud as a gunshot in the silence. They paused once more on the threshold, but there was no sound. There was no time for further caution. They had to move. They had escaped the basement but they were still in danger. Jenna knew that Kane had hunted the other women down before he had killed them. He could hunt them, too, when he returned and found them missing.

"We need to keep moving," she said to Keara.

Keara nodded, but she didn't speak. As they moved through the house, Jenna had to help support Keara. They made their way outside and staggered across the yard toward the dark, concealing woods.

Limping on bare feet slowed them down, but they had to ignore the pain. They were in an open, exposed place when they heard a car approaching. A moment later, headlights were probing the woods to their right. They dropped to the ground. When the headlights were gone, they ran again.

They ran straight into a wire fence. "Go over," Jenna said breathlessly, helping Keara climb a sagging section of the fence. Keara had to work her way carefully over several strands of barbed wire and Jenna followed her, wincing at a deep scratch on her arm as she dropped to the other side. She landed hard on the ground.

Jenna could hear her own breath as it rasped through her lungs. Keara was having an even harder time. Jenna realized that Keara wasn't in any condition to go on. They weren't nearly far enough to get them safely away.

The barn loomed out of the shadows to their right. It was the only way. She hurried Keara towards the barn and hid her in the hay inside. She would lead Kane away and hope that his fear of snakes would keep him from searching the barn. When she found help, she would come back for Keara.

Jenna started off into the woods once again. She tripped over rocks and roots and she fell into a hole she didn't see in the darkness. As she got up again, she head heavy footsteps in the brush behind her. She had to stifle her cry as she cut her foot on something sharp. What it was, she didn't know.

Branches lashed at her painfully, tearing at her flesh and her clothing. She caught her foot on a tangle of vines and went down again. She dragged herself up and stumbled forward again while her breath burned in her lungs. But she kept going. Kane was getting closer.

She ran, desperate now and almost blind with fear until she couldn't hear Kane pursuing her anymore. She plunged recklessly ahead into the darkness and kept going until she almost ran straight off a steep embankment.

She stopped herself just in time and heard a shower of gravel and rocks going over the edge. She saw the glimmer of moonlight on water below her. She couldn't go back the way she had come. She knew that her only escape was straight down.

She dropped down over the edge of the embankment and immediately began sliding down to the water below. She grasped desperately at branches, frantically trying to slow herself down. But she fell so fast that she almost sprawled headlong into the creek at the bottom.

The water was shallow enough. It reached only her calves, but the current was strong. It pulled at her legs as she made her way across the creek. Her bare feet slipped on the slick rocks on the bottom.

Kane was near again, she realized with sudden panic. She could hear him rustling the brush not far behind her. Somehow he had caught up with her.

Before she could make her exhausted body respond to the imminent threat behind her, she felt a hand clamp down on her shoulder. A sharp jerk pulled her towards the ground. She started to struggle but strong arms pulled her close.

"Shhh," she heard the low murmur against her hair. The whisper of warm breath swept her skin. A hand smoothed her hair. There was a leap in her chest as she heard her name.

She turned. The muscles of his chest were like steel beneath her grasping fingers. She leaned close and almost sobbed as she rasped out a single word. "Jesse."

Epilogue

Jesse was begging for mercy. Helplessly pinned on the ground, he tried to defend himself, but he wasn't having much luck against the onslaught of dog kisses.

When he was finally able to get free, he rose on one knee, made a mighty effort and grabbed the football. He sliced a pass over to Josh who caught it hard against his chest.

Abby was calling for the ball. Josh tossed it over to her. She caught it and ran, laughing as Max and Tasha surrounded her. It was more like a game of keep-away-from-the-dogs than football, and the dogs were having just as much fun as they were.

Their play was a little rough for Jenna right now. She watched them a few minutes longer through the kitchen window. A smile touched her face as she listened to the laughter. In their new yard. In their new house. In a new town.

Those weren't the only new things they had begun together. Jenna smoothed the top over her swollen abdomen and felt a hard kick. She kneaded her back for a few moments, and after the pain subsided, added another meal to the stack of dinners in the freezer. She heard the timer go off on the clothes dryer but knew there wouldn't be time to put the clothes away.

There was a soft breeze blowing through the window. It was a perfect day, she thought. *Friday's child is loving and giving.*

She walked to the back door, set her suitcase down, and then pushed the screen door open and stepped out onto the porch. She felt the sunshine, golden and clean, warming her. She smelled freshly-mown grass. She looked at the roses Jesse had planted that morning beside the trellis he had put up last week. The garden was three times the size of the garden she'd had in Alder Grove. The man liked working in his yard.

She hadn't told him yet. Two weeks of false labor pains and one trip to the hospital already had made her decide to keep the contractions to herself for the past few hours. But this was different.

She opened the screen door that opened into the backyard. "Jesse," she called. "It's time."

Jesse looked up. Jenna waited, smiling as she watched her husband drop the football and come running to the house.

the end

OTHER BOOKS BY SIARA BRANDT
AUTUMN OF THE WOLF
A RESTLESS WIND
BLOOD OATH: THE DRAGON'S CLAW
DARK OF PEACE
INTO NIGHT
STEALING CADY
RENDER SILENT
THE PATRIOT REMNANT: RETURN TO FREEDOM
TANGLED VINES

THE ASHES AND THE ROSES
(A sweeping tale of the American Civil War)

Review from *THE ASHES AND THE ROSES*:

"Beautiful! I absolutely love everything about this book. To me it is a delightfully, artfully, wonderfully and thoroughly awesome read."

THE PHANTOM SERIES
THE HAUNTNG OF THE OPERA
SHADOW OF THE PHANTOM
MAN OF DARKNESS

Review from *THE HAUNTNG OF THE OPERA*:

"Oh wow!!! This was a re-imagining that caught me by surprise. I downloaded it because I like Phantom fiction but this one caught me by the feels going on like a snapping turtle. I would recommend it to anyone with a Phantom in their heart and a lot of time to set aside to read. This is one of those books where after I pay the rent this is my first purchase. Bills be damned!"

THE DEADRISE SERIES (ZOMBIES!)
BLOOD SCOURGE: PROJECT DEADRISE
BLOOD STORM: DEADRISE II
SAVAGE BLOOD: DEADRISE III
BLOOD RECKONING: DEADRISE IV
BLOOD MOON: DEADRISE V
BLOOD CURSE: DEADRISE VI
BLOOD LUST: DEADRISE VII

Review for *BLOOD SCOURGE*:

"Great read. The book was very interesting. The characters were believable. I really liked Grey and Savhanna. I liked the fact that the author related to the reader the cause of the outbreak. The book came together well at the end but I found myself wanting to read more. Wanting to wish the characters good luck. I would recommend this book. Well worth the money."

Ms. Brandt defies the rules and writes books in a wide scope of genres, everything from suspenseful thrillers to horror stories to passionate romances (although there is *always* a tempestuous romance woven through each story no matter what its genre.) Whatever your mood, there is a book just for you!

To see other books by Siara Brandt, visit https://siarabrandt.wordpress.com/ and check out her blog. And if you join Siara Brandt's mailing list, you will receive her monthly newsletter where you will find the latest news on upcoming titles, excerpts, special promotions and giveaways.

Your opinion is important to us. Help other readers find these books by writing a review at your favorite book site, review sit, blog or your own social media.

It is my sincere wish that you have enjoyed reading this book. I hope that we find each other again soon in the pages of another adventure. –Siara

Siara Brandt has had a life-long obsession with writing. She is the author of over twenty novels. Just like the Giza Pyramids are located in the exact center of the geological land mass, she makes her home in almost the exact center of the United States where she shares a home with a fluctuating number of children, grandchildren and pets. She loves hearing from her readers. You can visit her at https://siarabrandt.wordpress.com/

Made in the USA
Columbia, SC
11 February 2023

11718898R00107